Journey to Forever

Also by Carol Steward in Large Print:

This Time Forever
Finding Amy

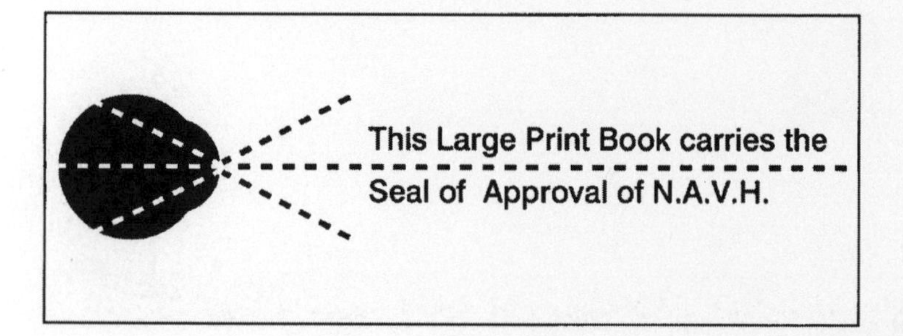

Journey to Forever

Carol Steward

Thorndike Press • Waterville, Maine

All characters in this book have no existence outside the imagination of the author and have no relation whatsoever to anyone bearing the same name or names. They are not even distantly inspired by any individual known or unknown to the author, and all incidents are pure invention.

Published in 2006 by arrangement with Harlequin Books S.A.

Thorndike Press® Large Print Christian Romance.

The text of this Large Print edition is unabridged.
Other aspects of the book may vary from the original edition.

Set in 16 pt. Plantin by Al Chase.

Printed in the United States on permanent paper.

Library of Congress Cataloging-in-Publication Data

Steward, Carol.
Journey to forever / by Carol Steward.
p. cm. — (Thorndike Press large print Christian romance)
ISBN 0-7862-8546-X (lg. print : hc : alk. paper)
1. Women journalists — Fiction. 2. Large type books.
I. Title. II. Thorndike Press large print Christian romance series.
PS3619.T493J68 2006
813′.6—dc22 2006001058

To Bette,
who has been my spiritual mentor
and always my dear friend!
And to my family,
for all your love and support.

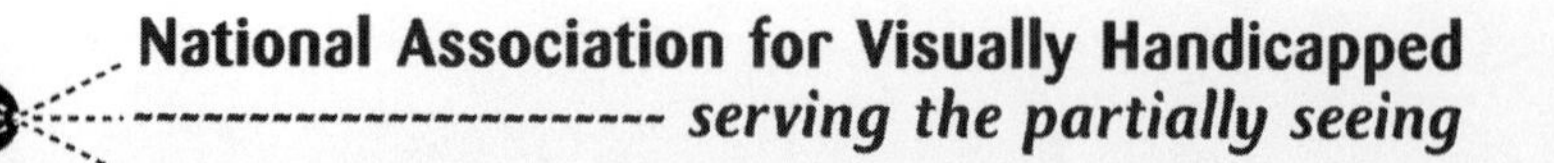

As the Founder/CEO of NAVH, the only national health agency solely devoted to those who, although not totally blind, have an eye disease which could lead to serious visual impairment, I am pleased to recognize Thorndike Press* as one of the leading publishers in the large print field.

Founded in 1954 in San Francisco to prepare large print textbooks for partially seeing children, NAVH became the pioneer and standard setting agency in the preparation of large type.

Today, those publishers who meet our standards carry the prestigious "Seal of Approval" indicating high quality large print. We are delighted that Thorndike Press is one of the publishers whose titles meet these standards. We are also pleased to recognize the significant contribution Thorndike Press is making in this important and growing field.

Lorraine H. Marchi, L.H.D.
Founder/CEO
NAVH

* Thorndike Press encompasses the following imprints: Thorndike, Wheeler, Walker and Large Print Press.

You whom I took from the ends of the earth and called you from its farthest corners, saying to you, "You are my servant, I have chosen you and not cast you off;" fear not, for I am with you, be not dismayed, for I am your God. I will strengthen you, I will help you, I will uphold you with my victorious right hand.

— *Isaiah* 41:9–10

Chapter One

Colin loosened the knot of his tie and glanced around the elaborately decorated office, pacing the floor as if it were a bad day in the dugout. He couldn't imagine why his new employer wanted to meet him away from the radio station.

Ellis Chapman sauntered through the entrance and extended his hand. "Nice to see you again, Colin. How's the shoulder recovering?"

"I finished therapy last month. It will never be able to take the rigors of baseball again, but it's doing fine, thanks." He had met the staunch icon of the community at several media functions over the years, before the career-ending rotator-cuff surgery forced him off the field. From there, he had moved into a temporary sports-announcing job, where he'd discovered his life's dream — spreading God's word over the sound waves.

"And the job? Is it what you thought it would be?"

When he became bored with sitting on the sidelines during the off-season of baseball, Colin had accepted Chapman's invitation to host a Christian radio show, where the spiritual and emotional challenges provided unexpected rewards on a daily basis. "I'm not missing sports nearly as much as I feared I might."

His boss grasped Colin's hand and enthusiastically pumped his arm. "Good," he said, motioning for Colin to follow him into his private office. Colin sank into the soft leather chair and waited for the point of the meeting to surface. "I've been meaning to talk to you about one of the topics you discussed on your show. We have a few skeptics in the community who think Christian broadcasting is no place for a retired baseball player. I think you've opened a lot of eyes to the fact that there are Christians everywhere, even in professional sports."

Feeling as if there was more Mr. Chapman had to say, Colin straightened his back, suddenly thankful for the privacy. If he was going to be fired, he didn't want an audience.

Before Colin could cut in Ellis added, "I have an interesting proposition for you."

That didn't sound too promising. Anything that started with *interesting* had to mean trouble. He was likely being demoted to the minor leagues of radio. Whatever that meant, Colin wasn't interested in another career change.

Mr. Chapman rambled on about needing to boost the ratings for the radio and the readership for the newspaper. Apparently advertising had dipped into the danger zones on both.

"We need to do something to grab the audience, and timing is critical. The board has been tossing about ideas, which brought you to mind."

Colin decided Mr. Chapman must have listened to his talk on "Financial Responsibility for Christians." He supposed he didn't blame him for doing what he had to do in order to keep his acquisitions in the black. Cutbacks were common with the economy in a slump. Three years ago, the *Denver Gazette* had been on the verge of bankruptcy. Ellis Chapman had bought it and turned it around, adding newspaper publishing to his communications conglomerate. *Failure* wasn't in Chapman's vocabulary and Colin highly respected him.

Chapman's assistant slipped into the room and quietly filled crystal goblets with sparkling water. "Pardon the interruption, Mr. Chapman. Miss Post's car broke down and she's going to be late. She sent her apologies."

Chapman shook his head, but his expression indicated he truly cared about the misfortune of the woman, whoever she was. "Thank you." He stood, stuffing his hands into his trouser pockets as he paced the room in silence.

Colin watched, his patience tested. How will I fit into Chapman's plan? He realized the world of Christian radio might not appreciate his unconventionality, from his shaved head to his high-profile and highly competitive career. He knew it seemed unlikely that a believer could remain faithful when hit with so many temptations in the limelight. He'd learned long ago that the best way to avoid false accusations was to keep focused on the Lord. He couldn't let doubt throw him a curveball now. "I have to admit, your call piqued my curiosity. Is there a concern with my work?" Colin's question caught Mr. Chapman's attention.

Was that humor Colin saw in Ellis's expression?

"Oh, no. As I mentioned, Colin, your show got me thinking about this younger generation. I listened to your discussion about commitment to giving in the community and took the tape to the board for their opinion. Which is why I've called you here today. I guarantee this is right up your alley." Chapman, who was nearly as round as he was tall, leaned against the giant desk in his office. "I recall your name being tied to several fund-raisers during your baseball career."

Colin tugged at his tie, recalling the antics he had performed to raise money for charity. "Sir, I don't follow you. Do those pose a problem?"

"If there is anyone who can make news out of something so prosaic, it's you, Colin. And what absolutely galls me is the success you have doing it." A smile crinkled his round face.

"Prosaic?" Not exactly a compliment. "What does that have to do with anything?"

"Your stunts were absolutely mundane tasks anyone could do, yet you drew the audience right in with you. Who would have ever thought pushing a peanut down the Sixteenth Street Mall with your nose or sitting in every seat of every professional ballpark in the country would bring in thousands of dollars? It shows that all of us can do something to help those in need."

"Has someone just found out about this? You had to have known my willingness to make a fool of myself for charity's sake before the board agreed to hire me. I happen to find helping others rewarding," he said, unable to keep the anger out of his voice.

"Calm down. You've got it all wrong. What we want to know is if you're ready for another stunt." He explained that the executive board had voted unanimously to ask Colin.

Relief washed over him. "That's what all of this is about?"

"That's it. Every year we do something to get involved with the community. We buy school supplies, coat drives, collect bedding, the usual. But this year, we want to boost our exposure and do something that will make a lasting impression on the community, so we'd like something with a bit of pizzazz. We immediately thought of you, if you're willing."

"What do you have in mind?"

"Actually, we're considering drawing the audience into that decision, if you're game. We'll give them two weeks to come up with the best stunt idea and they'll win a prize. The board is meeting here in a few minutes, in fact. I'd like you to be here."

It had been three years since his last stunt, and it had taken months for his body to recover from that one. He'd been in shape then. How difficult would it be now that he was no longer on a training schedule?

"That's fine. When is the big event?"

A deep laugh rolled from Chapman's chest as he stood and paced the perimeter of the room. "That depends on the event itself. But we'd like it sooner rather than later. I want the public to see you, to watch you and to be able to cheer you on. We need them to connect with this project."

"Where is the money going?" Colin heard female voices outside Chapman's office door.

"Several agencies have approached us for donations, but I'm leaning toward Good Samaritan . . ." Ellis said just as the striking blonde blew into the room like a tornado in search of a target.

"It's dead! Just blew a water pump and some head gas thingies right in the middle of the mousetrap."

Colin cringed at the thought of breaking down on the worst highway maze in the city.

"I can't believe I drove that jalopy. . . ." She brushed the silky hair from her eyes and dropped into the chair, flying back to her feet immediately when she landed on Colin instead of the plush leather. Her eyes widened when she spun around and looked at him. "Oh dear."

Colin didn't know what to say or do.

"I didn't see you," she said, backing

away. She glanced at Mr. Chapman and covered her mouth with her hand. "I'm so sorry."

"No harm done," Colin said, wondering if she was always so easily flustered.

"I didn't think the meeting had started yet . . ." Her fair complexion turned a rosy pink. "I, uh, I'm sorry I interrupted." A quick glance at her watch brought a frown and she pulled her sleeve back over the shiny silver band.

He knew he shouldn't stare, but he had no choice. Her pastel blue pants were badly wrinkled and smudged with dirt. Frustration flashed in her ice-blue eyes. He stood and extended a hand. "I'm Colin Wright. Mr. Chapman and I were just discussing a few things, you didn't interrupt."

She clasped his hand briefly and whispered hello, all the while eyeing him with a calculating expression.

Mr. Chapman cut her off before she had a chance to introduce herself, though even without the verbal notes, Colin had already concluded from her confusion and the smears of black grease on her chin that she was the unfortunate Miss Post.

"This is Nicole Post, an intern at the *Gazette*. I've suggested she might want to sit in on the board meeting, see another side of the business. Why don't you take a minute to freshen up, Nicole, and we'll meet you in the boardroom."

She looked young and energetic, even if her car wasn't. Both her energy and an unreliable vehicle were typical of a college student, though she appeared slightly older and more mature than the traditional coed, though her actions called that into question.

"I'll be back as soon as possible." She backed her way to the door, trying to avoid looking at Colin.

Her embarrassment made his heart beat a little quicker. When their eyes met, he smiled. He should know better than to try to convince himself that he was simply being a gentleman by ignoring her inappropriate behavior. In most situations, barging into the CEO's office would be an automatic strikeout, not to mention sitting on an associate's lap, accident or not. Still, there was an innocence about Nicole Post that intrigued him.

As quickly as the thought entered his mind, he reminded himself that it would be career suicide to consider flirting with a fellow employee, even if they were in different branches.

Nikki rushed into the nearest ladies' room

and locked the door behind her. "I can't believe I just waltzed into the office throwing such a tantrum that I didn't even notice a gorgeous man sitting there," she mumbled. She lathered her face and scrubbed the greasy smudges from her cheeks with paper towels then splashed her face with water and touched up her foundation. There was no need to add blush, Mother Nature had given her an abundance of that already.

She wiped the wrinkled trousers with a damp towel and straightened the linen suit as her mind flashed back to Colin's smile. Unbuttoning the jacket so it wouldn't hug her derriere, Nikki glanced at her hair and dismissed the idea of making an impression on anyone, let alone a popular public figure like Colin. His deep-set smoky blue eyes had taken her breath away, and he probably knew it from the twitch of the muscle hidden beneath his five o'clock shadow. She glanced at her watch, realizing it wasn't even noon, so his whiskers were an intentional look. That figures, she thought. He's a hometown kid riding the wave of his brief encounter with notoriety. Today's news, tomorrow's heartbreak. Nikki tossed her head and raised her chin.

She slipped into the boardroom as the discussion turned to publicity. Finding only one seat left, across from Colin, Nikki felt him watching her as she sat.

Colin spoke quite eloquently for a baseball player, she decided as he agreed to participate in the fund-raiser.

She couldn't believe the board had actually agreed to Colin representing them. Just a few months ago, they weren't even convinced it was a good decision to have a professional athlete on the air. Publicity stunts were juvenile and immature. Surely the conservative board would veto the entire idea before someone took it seriously.

"I appreciate your offer to help, Colin dear, but I don't think a Christian radio station should have to resort to frivolous stunts to bring in an income," Mrs. Franklin said with her hands folded in her lap.

Nikki was pleased with the comment, suddenly realizing this might not have been Colin's idea. If he hadn't proposed the idea, who had? Was Chapman Communications in financial trouble?

The advertising manager shook his head. "We're not keeping the money, Mrs. Franklin. It's going to a charity. We benefit from the exposure, not the income."

Nikki let out a mental sigh of relief.

A heated discussion about the impropriety of the idea broke out again, leaving she and Colin watching the arguments volley from pro to con.

"If I might add something here," Colin interrupted. "Ever since September 11, non-profit organizations have suffered a terrible blow, as has our country. Efforts to help the victims were quite generous, and now it seems the public and the victims are ready to shift their attention to other needs that still exist elsewhere."

Around the table, Nikki watched heads nod.

"Whether the task seems trivial or not doesn't seem to matter. Pushing a peanut down the Sixteenth Street Mall with my nose raised $612,000 for medical research. Stadium-sitting raised nearly eight hundred thousand. Parachuting onto the pitcher's mound made a couple of hundred thousand for medical bills for a leukemia patient. We can't begin to underestimate the generosity of our community. I'm sure this will light a fire for giving."

Nikki managed to subdue her shock at the total of Colin's efforts, though she instinctively glanced in his direction.

The director of publicity interjected more astounding and unbelievable facts. "Colin's stunts raised nearly two million dollars in the aggregate. It may not make any sense to all of us, but that isn't the point. We need something to garner more attention for the newspaper and the radio station while raising money for those in need. We should set an example for the community to follow."

Nikki's attention wandered to the man across from her. Colin didn't even have the decency to argue the embellishment. How could anyone have raised that much money if there wasn't something in it for him?

"I believe Colin can help us meet that goal, as well as raise money for the homeless shelter at the same time."

Something in the conversation finally provoked a reaction from Colin. His dark brows furrowed, accentuating his receding hairline. "Homeless shelter?"

"Yes, Good Sam Shelter. Didn't I tell you that?"

Leaning his elbows on the mahogany table, Colin matched fingertips on both hands and shrugged slightly. "I'm sure you did. I must have missed the details, I guess." He seemed irritated by the information.

"That isn't a problem, is it?" Nikki asked, to the surprise of everyone there, including herself. The words were out of her mouth before she realized it.

Colin's tan looked considerably paler

than it had ten minutes ago. Despite the odd expression, he shook his head. "No. I can't think of a more worthy cause."

Nikki determined then and there that she was going to find out the truth behind Colin's reaction.

Chapter Two

Colin couldn't help but wonder if his past had finally caught up with the media. He wanted out.

Out of the room and out of this commitment. Now, before Miss I-Know-You-Have-a-Secret Post plastered her suspicions across the front page of the paper. He inhaled slowly, carefully freezing his face in a confident smile.

She hadn't actually rolled her eyes at the ideas posed during the discussion, but she had yawned more than once. Still, her smile seemed to brighten with his slip of the tongue. Maybe it was her eyes. Did eyes smile and taunt, like heartless children making fun of little boys when their lives fell apart?

Don't be ridiculous, Colin. She's just an intern, not a reporter.

Nothing had stopped him from helping others before. No one had ever questioned why he'd agreed to participate in any of the previous fund-raisers. He glanced back at Miss Post, feeling like her next meal. She had barely taken her eyes off him the entire meeting.

Journalists need to get a life of their own, he thought. Suddenly he had braces again and Molly with the big brown eyes and curly blond pigtails was staring at him, and he had the strongest urge to make a face, just like he had in fifth grade, when he decided girls were the worst invention God had ever made.

He looked back at Nicole, realizing how innocently right his thinking had been. God had created Eve as a helpmate, but she'd turned out to be a temptress, responsible for Adam's fall. How many times would it take before he learned — beauty is only skin-deep?

When would the Lord introduce him to a woman whose heart led her life? One who didn't care if he ended up in a homeless shelter, as long as they were together. Not that he ever planned to let his life get so far out of control, but still, every day the unexpected happened to those who least expected it. Did such a woman even exist?

Colin smiled and waited for Nicole to glance his way again. It was the closest he could manage to making faces. Especially at this woman. Her broken-down car and a little grime did little to disguise her graceful poise and flippant attitude. He could feel his expression moving toward an unflattering scowl when Colin heard his name.

"Personally, I don't think we should take time for a contest to choose the events for a stunt. If the shelter is overcrowded now, surely we can come up with something Colin is willing to do. What if Colin walks across the state?" Mrs. Franklin asked in her shaky voice.

"Every organization sponsors walks." Chapman's smile disappeared as he leaned back in the leather chair and tossed out other stunt ideas, none of which impressed Colin.

"Pocketbooks are a lot thinner these days. And face it, Colin, the public expects more from you. The more outrageous the better."

"I agree, but I'm not pushing a peanut across the state. If we only do a ten mile walk, the event will be out of the public's mind in a matter of an hour or two," Colin said adamantly. "The focus of this should be on the needs of the homeless. Many of them live in their cars, or sell them for money to put food on the table forcing them to take alternative methods of transportation. I like the border-to-border idea."

Mr. Chapman's assistant handed the publisher and each board member a packet on homeless families, suggesting everyone take time to peruse the statistics and send

Mr. Chapman ideas. Colin felt memories return as he glanced at the pictures in the brochure. He felt perspiration on his forehead.

"Do you really think this is a good time for this?" Colin asked.

Ellis rubbed his hand over his clean-shaven chin. "Trust me," Ellis said with emphasis, "this issue is a magnet right now. Anything you do in the name of this proposed shelter will draw attention."

More ideas crossed the table before the meeting officially closed. Colin and Mr. Chapman walked back toward his office. "I'm sure we can come up with something creative," Chapman stated.

Colin paused at the assistant's desk, expecting to schedule another meeting. "This promotion is a great idea, and I'm glad to be part of it." Colin could feel God's hand taking control of the project even as they spoke. Even in the crevices of his memories, going through with this didn't seem quite as frightening as it had an hour ago with Nicole Post staring him down like a head-hunting pitcher.

Chapman motioned Colin to his office. "Unless you have someplace else to be, why don't we continue the discussion now?"

"Now is fine," Colin said, knowing better

than to tell his boss no. Unless he were meeting with the President of the United States, nothing had better be more important than hearing what his boss had to say.

"Let's consider how to go about this. As you said, homeless people often sell everything, even their cars, to get by. What if you don't use any motorized vehicle during the journey? What if you make the trip on a pogo stick, or a scooter?" Ellis jotted notes, then shook his head. "Wait. Are those the contraptions with those obnoxiously loud motors?"

"I believe so," Colin said.

"That's out then." He scribbled a note, then looked at Colin again.

He could almost see Ellis's brain working to come up with a preposterous mode of transportation to keep public interest. "I may as well get my neighbor's son's tricycle to make the trip."

Mr. Chapman's eyes lit. "Now you're thinking!"

"I beg your pardon, Mr. Chapman. I was joking."

"Call me Ellis. And I'm not. Look at the attention you'd get if every day of the journey you use a different mode of transportation. One day a nonmotorized scooter — I bought one of those for each of my grandchildren one Christmas." He laughed, obviously recalling something about the holiday.

"My sister broke her wrist using hers."

"Maybe we should reconsider. We don't want any injuries."

"I don't think we have anything to worry about. She won't be joining us, and I had no problem with mine."

"Good. Another day you could take roller skates. We need something to really catch the eye."

Colin scratched his chin. Ellis had a point. "I'm not trying to be difficult, but are we talking from the east to west borders of the state? I'm game for a few different methods of getting there, to a limit, but I don't think anything except bicycles are allowed on I-70 through the majority of the mountains."

"We'll have to work with the Department of Transportation on that." He pressed his intercom and asked his secretary to connect him with someone in that government agency. A few minutes later he finished a discussion with the man and turned back to Colin. "Colorado Department of Transportation won't even consider it on I-70, but they felt we could work something out going south to north. Not all of it could be on the interstate, but there are several sections where foot traffic and bicycles are allowed. If we contact this guy once we have a plan, he'll push the permission through."

Colin was impressed. They discussed the personnel needs for the project, how quickly they could pull it all together, and how soon to start publicizing. A lightbulb flashed on. "How about naming it the 'Back on Track Relay'?"

"Relay? Oh, I see, not a relay where the people change with each leg, but one where the 'event' itself would change. I love it!" Mr. Chapman slapped Colin on the back.

"I think this is going to be my best money-maker yet," Colin enthused.

"Why don't we guarantee it? How about if I double the pledges if you finish the trip without any motorized vehicle in a week?"

Double? He held out his right hand. "Deal."

"Not so quickly. We need to iron out a few more details."

Colin pulled his hand slowly to his body. "Such as?"

"I'd like my own crew, from the paper, to report every step of the way."

A watchdog, Colin thought. That shouldn't have surprised him, either, but it did irritate him. He felt certain God would provide for this project, he couldn't start doubting His plan already. "Don't forget, we do have some issues to iron out with the Department of Transportation, and I'm sure that the larger the procession the more problems we're going to run into getting clearance," Colin said.

"I'll keep it small. One or two people, max," Ellis said with a smile. "In the meantime, you'd better start training again. Who knows how long it will take CDOT to approve the highway permissions. I know they'll move as fast as they can, but we need to be ready when it comes through. And, as you know, it would be wise for you to spend some time at the shelter to get to know the full scope of the project." Ellis walked around his desk and offered a hand.

Colin stood, sensing their meeting was over. "I'll be sure to make arrangements to do that," he said, confident that he wouldn't learn anything about the situation that he didn't already know by heart.

Chapter Three

Pushing a peanut down Denver's Sixteenth Street Mall was a far cry from walking across the state from New Mexico to Wyoming. Colin wanted to be prepared for anything.

"You've been on that cycle for almost an hour now. What's the scoop?" His bodybuilder buddy eyed Colin suspiciously. "You're not up to another of your hare-brained stunts, are you?"

Colin rubbed the soft stubble on his scalp and laughed. He'd spent two weeks trying to figure out how to break the news to his best friend. Another week and he would find out about it, along with the public, and Colin would never hear the end of it. He may as well get it over with now. "Hare-brained — no. Fund-raiser — yes."

"I thought sitting in fifty-five thousand stadium seats had brought you to your senses," Jared said, sitting on the stationary cycle next to Colin's.

"My quads seem to have forgotten about that. And right now isn't a good time to remind me. I'm already committed to the fund-raiser. It's not even an option to back out."

Jared laughed. "Right, like you would if you could. No offense meant, but you never walk if you can run. Never drive if you can ride . . ."

"Point made already." He didn't need to hear a full listing of the childhood pranks they'd pulled, not to mention the publicity stunts he was so well-known for. God hadn't wired him to sit still, especially when there was something to be done.

Jared crossed his arms over his chest and groaned. "Seriously, Colin. I haven't seen you here in a long time. You don't want to overdo it."

"I play roller hockey every week with no problems. Don't worry, I'm feeling great."

"So, how long do we have to get you ready?"

"I'm not sure. I'd like to wait until the temperatures are out of the hundreds, at least. September would be just about right."

Jared looked at the readout on the cycle and shrugged. "Not a bad time for someone who hasn't been to the gym in over a year. And what's the cause this time?"

Colin hesitated, but knew he had to get ready to face the public with his support. "A new homeless shelter."

Jared's eyes opened wide.

"The existing downtown shelter has been overbooked for two years," Colin said before Jared could expound on his reaction.

"Whose idea was the shelter?"

"Chapman Communications's board. What could I say? He's my boss."

Jared's almost silent click of the tongue confirmed that he knew Colin had really jumped at the opportunity. "You're kinda between a rock and a hard place with the boss then, aren't you? And I don't suppose you considered . . ."

Colin ignored his friend's dubious expression. "I'll work through it. I'm hoping you'll come along to keep me going."

"Keep you going?" Jared said in surprise. "Just how far is it this time?"

He hadn't added the mileage up completely, he hated to admit. "We're still working on permission from the Colorado Department of Transportation, so I don't have an exact figure yet . . ."

"The Department of Transportation!" Jared whacked him on the shoulder. "What are you thinking?"

"Suffice it to say, it's a lot more than ten miles. I estimate roughly three hundred and twenty-five miles, depending on how much we can travel on the interstate and how much we have to take side roads."

Jared barely let him get the sentence out. "Have you forgotten the reason your baseball career really ended? The one you kept quiet? Asthma is nothing to ignore."

At least Jared had the decency to lower his voice so there was no chance anyone else could hear. "I haven't had any recurrences in four years." Colin looked around the gym when Jared stood, noticing that the patrons were clearing out as the workday started. "The doctor never even confirmed it was an asthma attack. If I wasn't willing to endanger my life for baseball, you know I wouldn't risk it for anything else. Look, I'm having no problems." Colin took a deep breath and forced it out without any problems. "See, I'm cured."

"Have you totally lost your mind? Your own well-being aside, raising money for a homeless shelter is a touchy issue these days. Haven't you read all of the letters to the editor lately?"

"Of course I've read them. Why do you think I'm doing this? Someone has to do more than complain about the problem. It isn't going away."

"This isn't like the money you raised for cancer research, Colin," Jared stated as he handed Colin a water bottle. "Who could argue the nobility of that? Unfortunately, society doesn't look at the homeless person in the same way as it does a sick person."

Colin guzzled the water while Jared spouted off his objection to the project. "You don't have to remind me of that, either. It's a perfect opportunity to educate the public. No one is immune to this problem."

"You aren't worried that someone will find out that you lived in a shelter? Your dad didn't handle it well at the time. I doubt he would appreciate you bringing it up again."

"I don't relish the idea of revisiting that time, but I explained it to Dad already. He's hoping it doesn't have to become public knowledge, either, but he understands it will help others in need, so he's supporting me in my decision. It was twenty years ago and I was eleven, after all," Colin said with a shrug. It was the fear of upsetting his family's lives that worried him, but he knew it would be callous of him to let his past stand in the way of helping those in need. "This is just as important as any other epidemic. More and more families have become victims of the economy. On my first visit to the shelter I met a couple who had gone through the husband's battle with cancer, only to be evicted from their home when he'd barely been released from the hospital. What kind of a landlord would kick a sick man's family out?"

"We don't know what the landlord had been through."

Colin nodded. "I shouldn't be so idealistic, I know. But I can't help feeling sympathy for those families who move from place to place to put a roof over their heads. The public complains about people sleeping in the parks and on the streets, so we've come up with a possible solution."

"How are we supposed to keep up with the growing need? We can't just keep building more shelters. All around you hear about problems with people abusing the systems that are trying to help them." Jared grabbed the spray bottle of disinfectant and the terry-cloth towel and wiped down the vacant equipment next to Colin.

"It's not a perfect system, but we're trying to help. Even if I can't stop the injustices, I can't leave people to sleep in the parks. We have to do something!"

"We?" Jared shook his head then laughed and held up his hands in defeat. "I have yet to figure out what drives you to do these crazy things, but you know I'm not about to miss the fun."

"Glad to keep you so entertained." The

stationary cycle came to a steep hill setting and Colin stopped talking just long enough to work his muscles through the burn. A comfortable silence encompassed the room, broken only by the soft whirr of the exercise machines. Colin enjoyed today's workout and wondered why he'd stopped coming. Had it been the injury, or was that simply an excuse? He loved the old warehouse that Jared and Sandra had renovated. The gym overlooked the South Platte River, the city's largest amusement park and on a clear day he could even enjoy a view of the Rocky Mountains. All that, and the gym wasn't far from Colin's loft apartment in the newly fashionable lower downtown, or "LoDo" area. He had no good excuse for not working out more often.

"On a lighter note," Jared interrupted Colin's peaceful retreat. "We're having a Fourth of July barbecue and Sandra is inviting a few friends." He crossed his formidable arms across his chest and feigned innocence. They both knew his wife was itching to find Colin another girlfriend.

Colin inhaled deeply, preparing for the imposing hill ahead on the simulated bike trail. "I'm busy, but thanks anyway."

"Busy, or not ready?"

"Both." Colin knew he shouldn't hold it

against anyone else that his ex-girlfriend had expected him to spend every penny of his savings on an engagement ring. His blood pressure went up every time he thought about it. For that amount he could have furnished his entire loft and had some left for a rainy day. As painful as it was to learn they had different attitudes about what was important in life, Colin was thankful for the incident. Friends and family had warned him about her exclusive tastes and indulgences. It was his own fault that he had chosen to ignore their concern until it was nearly too late.

"It's been almost a year," Jared reminded him. "Besides, you-know-who's not even invited." Colin had tried for months to convince himself that just because she'd been a friend of Jared and Sandra's, it didn't mean all of their friends were the same.

"I certainly hope not," Colin said, trying not to sound bitter. "She's moved to where the 'real' money is."

"Oh," Jared said. "Then there's nothing to stop you from coming. You're not my only single friend, and there aren't just single women coming, either."

Colin's eyes opened wide and he looked at Jared. "I can find my own dates when I'm ready. Thanks anyway."

"That came out all wrong. I meant we have married couples coming, too. Happily married. And a few singles. The purpose of our barbecue is not to set you up, okay?"

Colin shook his head. "You can stop while you're ahead. I'm working that day, but thanks for the invitation." After a few minutes, Jared gave up and left Colin alone to battle his own issues.

Across the room Colin noticed another tortured athlete taking revenge on the equipment. He glanced over to make sure Jared wasn't keeping too close a tab on him before taking another look at the woman. His friends meant well, but he simply wasn't ready to date again. Especially not if it meant being with another socialite like Bev.

Jared left the room, and Colin again admired the woman, getting the feeling that he had met her before. The very fact that she was here, at the most reasonably priced health club in LoDo, told him one thing about her, she appreciated a bargain. Her name-brand sweats and shoes looked soft from heavy use. He considered her choice of modest, well-worn sweats and T-shirt, which impressed him a lot more than the skintight leggings and equally revealing athletic tank tops many women wore. Obviously she didn't care what anyone thought. Her attention was focused on the view as her ponytail bounced in rhythm with the movement of her feet. A baseball cap hid her eyes.

He recalled his mother's disapproval of his usual choice in women, Bev in particular. Too thin, too fussy and only after his money. He guessed Mom's instincts had been right after all.

Colin glanced at the woman again. She'd mastered the orbital machine, the same one that had sent him flying like an uncoordinated geek the first and last time he'd tried it. She seemed to be concentrating on whatever was playing on her headphones instead of trying to impress anyone else. Why did she look so familiar?

The arrival of a few more customers stole his attention, saving him from making a fool of himself right here in front of Jared, who paused briefly to greet his customers then made a beeline to Colin.

"You've been riding for nearly ninety minutes. No need to overdo it the first day back." Jared said. "And since you've officially asked me to take care of you, check your pulse and take ten minutes to stretch before you leave."

Colin touched his index finger to his carotid artery and leaned forward to see the clock, conveniently located near the woman who had motivated him to ride half an hour longer than he'd planned, hoping for an opportunity to introduce himself.

Unfortunately, everyone in the gym pretty much kept to themselves. This was not the "in" place to meet available singles. Of course, in his college days, he hadn't needed to find a place to meet girls. They'd found him. He had been the only baseball player in the state to make it to the major leagues.

"Right on target," Colin said a few minutes later as he stretched. "I haven't turned into a couch potato just because I haven't been here, you know."

"Obviously not, or you'd be in real trouble about now. Hope to see you more often with your new project in mind. Make sure you let me know the dates so Sandra and I can put it on our calendars."

"I'll see you tomorrow. I should be able to give you more details then."

He showered, stopping to say goodbye to Jared on his way out, half wishing for another chance to run into the blonde, but she was long gone. "Think about the barbecue."

"I'll see what I can do." Colin didn't feel especially festive lately, and besides, the last thing he needed right now was the distraction of a woman.

Chapter Four

Colin's day had been dampened by another article in the morning *Gazette* about the group of home owners planning to fight the sale of property for the proposed shelter. Ever since Ellis made the public announcement, the editor had received a barrage of letters arguing for and against it. When Colin saw protesters marching outside the station, he felt as if monsoon season had broken loose over Denver. Mr. Chapman had to be pleased with the results of his plan so far. Papers were selling like never before.

After training for two months straight to get ready for the event, Colin would hate to see the project fall apart. He leaned heavily on Paul's advice to the Philippians — "He who began a good work in you will bring it to completion at the day of Jesus Christ." Keep the faith. God started this project, He'll see it through to the finish.

Despite the discouragement, Colin hoped Jared and Sandra's Labor Day party would cheer him up. He walked up the steps and rang the doorbell, not really expecting anyone to answer. With a lush yard like

Jared and Sandra's, there was no need to stay inside. Laughter spilled through the seams of the fence and Colin made his way around the house to the trellised gate. Their black Labrador Lizzy greeted Colin with her fierce bark. When Colin said hello, the dog gave him an embarrassed look and wagged her tail in welcome.

"Colin! I was afraid you were going to stand us up again," Sandra exclaimed, glancing at her watch. "Better late than never. The good news is there's plenty of food left, the baseball game is almost over, and you didn't miss the Rockies' fireworks display."

Heads turned and friends waved. He felt like a show-boater with Lizzy's bark and Sandra's booming voice announcing his late arrival. "Thanks. Looks like you've been busy."

"Can I fix you a plate?" Sandra was a hostess extraordinaire, a disgrace to the feminist movement, according to Colin's sister. The Hayes's barbecues were traditionally standing room only. Tonight was no exception.

"Don't worry about me, I'll make my way to the buffet table in a while."

Jared arrived with a tall glass of lemonade and yelled, "Forty-five minutes until showtime!"

Colin found an empty chair in a dark corner of the yard and sank into its cushions, fearful that he'd fall asleep and miss the fireworks display altogether. This last week he'd been pushing twenty miles a day. "Looks like you and Sandra outdid yourselves as usual."

"Yeah, too bad you . . ." Colin didn't hear another word Jared said. His attention fell on the blonde from the gym and he realized immediately where they'd met. With her scruffy workout clothes and baseball cap she had looked nothing like she had at the board meeting.

Jared followed Colin's gaze. "I didn't think you were interested in dating again."

"I'm not." Colin shrugged and shook his head. "I'm just surprised to see her here. Did you invite all of your patrons?"

Jared laughed. "No, but she's a regular. Let me introduce you."

Colin looked at her again, and their eyes met. She immediately lowered her chin and turned away, as if she didn't want to talk to him, either. "No thanks, I'm not interested in being set up." Which was exactly what had to be happening. What were the odds of running into the same woman three times in a couple of months without someone's intervention?

"Aren't you at least a little curious? She's not like the others, trust me. She's . . ."

"No offense, bud, but I'd be more interested in watching a documentary on ant migration." Colin ignored Jared's comment, heaved himself out of the chair and headed for the food, Lizzy close behind.

"I don't think ants migrate." Jared tossed his paper cup into the trash and blocked the stairs through the garden. "You don't understand . . ."

Colin glanced over his shoulder and noticed the woman walking toward Sandra. "Oh, too bad, she's leaving . . ." Colin said with quiet sarcasm. "Now can I eat?" He rushed to the table and started filling his plate with salads and warm barbecued ribs.

"She's not like Bev, or Robin . . ."

Colin tossed Lizzy a grape, watching her roll it around in her huge mouth as if it were a toy. "Do you see a pattern developing here, Jared?" Colin pushed his way past Jared and away from the woman. "You have a propensity for finding me women with expensive tastes and no heart."

"I beg to argue with you there," Jared said defensively.

Colin grabbed a handful of chips then reached for the ladle to add extra sauce to the ribs. "You already have the perfect wife.

Find me another Sandra, and I'll let you introduce us. Until then, I don't want a thing to do with another one of your rich friends."

Jared cleared his throat and popped open a soda tab. "Hi, honey. Hey, Nikki."

Colin didn't want to believe Jared would stoop so low as to be joking about this. "Nice try," he said to his friend, and turned, hearing Lizzy yip seconds before she lunged for his plate. Colin spun around to get it out of Lizzy's reach.

The plate crumpled against the blonde and the ladle flipped from his hand, splattering her head with warm barbecue sauce, sending it dripping down her beautiful face.

"Oh, no," Colin said, feeling the earth shift to slow motion. "I'm so, so sorry." He motioned to Lizzy, who was leading Jared on a wild scramble through the yard, ribs dangling from her mouth, sending guests in every direction. "I, uh, Lizzy . . . uh, that all happened so fast."

She leaned forward to let the sauce drip off her face and tugged her hair back into a ponytail. He wasn't totally sure if she was smiling or crying.

"Here are some napkins," Colin instinctively wiped the spicy sauce from her forehead, eyes and high cheekbones, overcome with an inkling to kiss it from her lips. Now that's a brilliant way to convince Jared that I'm not interested in romance.

"Let me get you a wet washcloth," Sandra said, right before she disappeared into the house.

"Ooh, it's burning my eyes," Nikki said, closing them tighter.

Colin grabbed another handful of napkins and started at the top of her face again. "I think this is going to take more than a washcloth, I'm sorry to say. Here, you have something on your lip." He was reaching up to pluck the piece of onion from her upper lip when she pursed her lips and blew it off, right onto Colin. He flinched, then started laughing. "Guess I had that coming."

She covered her mouth with her hand and her eyes blinked open, then she immediately closed them again. "Is there some water around? I really need to rinse my eyes."

"I'll help you inside. Sandra's probably getting a shower ready." He thought about the light-colored carpet and glanced again at the bright red sauce she wore from head to toe. "Slip your shoes off out here and I'll clean them while you shower."

He helped her balance while she blindly tugged the red leather mock cowboy boots off. Colin noted her tiny feet and slender ankles.

Sandra appeared just as he started to direct her through the door. "Here you go." She tucked the washcloth into Nikki's hand.

Colin looked at the mess he'd made and back at Sandra. "It's in her eyes and hair. Do you mind if she showers?"

"My thought exactly. I set towels out on the floor already, so come on in."

"Are you sure it's that bad? I need to be at work in an hour," Nikki said, still blinded.

"Trust us, you'll want to get that off as soon as possible." Sandra led her into the privacy of the master bath and Colin returned to the yard. Jared had finally retrieved the ribs from the dog and was examining her jaw.

"Is Liz okay?" Colin asked as he wiped the spatters from Nikki's boots.

"Yeah," Jared said from inside the fenced kennel. "I'm just making sure she didn't get any bone slivers stuck in her cheeks. Luckily I got all but one rib from her before she could eat more. I'm sorry about this."

"Who can blame her, the food smelled delicious."

Jared locked the kennel gate behind him, before saying goodbye to a departing couple. "Sorry to disrupt the party, everyone." He shrugged. "The fireworks should be starting any time now. Have a seat and enjoy." Despite the welcoming invitation, the guests expressed their thanks and left.

Colin and Jared carried food into the kitchen and put it away while they waited for Nicole to finish showering. The water ran and ran. Sandra spread the splotchy jeans across the kitchen table and started scrubbing. "I can't get them washed before she leaves, and mine won't fit her, so I'll just have to spot-clean them for now." She scrubbed until the only remnant was a wet circle or two. Then she threw them into the dryer. "Her blouse is ruined, and the jean jacket is probably history, too." Sandra heaved a sigh. "I can't believe Lizzy did such a thing."

They heard the water turn off and Sandra ran to the laundry room, then disappeared with Nikki's jeans. A few minutes later, both women returned. Nikki's silky hair was pulled to the top of her head in a ponytail and the whites of her eyes were beet-red. He wasn't sure if she'd been crying or if the hot-pepper seasoning had burned them, or both. Sandra asked Jared for a baseball cap.

"All of mine are old and d—" Jared began.

Colin interrupted. "I have some from the radio station in my car. Let me get you one." He ran to his vehicle and returned a few minutes later, wishing he could have done more to make the situation right. There were faded circles on her jeans where Sandra had scrubbed the barbecue sauce from the denim. Colin handed the cap to her.

"This seems a little out of order, but I thought I'd introduce you to Nikki Post," Sandra said.

"Yeah, we've met." He hoped she hadn't heard his remark about the women Jared had set him up with, or if she had, that she'd forgotten by now.

Nikki looked confused and more than a little wary. She didn't offer her hand in return. "Hello again." She slipped her feet into her boots, ignoring him.

He looked at both of the hosts, who were blatantly studying the interaction. "I'm really sorry about this, Nicole," he said, wishing someone would send him a lifeline from the awkward silence.

"It's Nikki."

He felt as if Jared had dumped a cooler full of ice-cold sports drink over his head. "It's a small world, Nikki. We seem destined to run into each other . . . literally. Please accept . . ."

Nikki's voice softened. "No need apologizing, accidents happen. Thanks for the clothes, Sandra. I won't have time to change before work, so I'll bring them back to you at the gym."

Despite her brush-off, he could at least make an attempt to be cordial. "You didn't happen to write the article on the homeless shelter in this morning's paper, did you?"

Her tanned skin turned pale. "No, I'm an intern, remember? I'm sure that went to Gary, our local reporter." She eased herself away just as the fireworks display started with a series of loud explosions and a shower of colorful sparks. Nikki paused to look. "I'm bouncing between proofreading and copyediting right now, so I don't write the articles."

Something didn't make sense. Why had an intern who was still proofreading attended a board meeting? "I see. How much longer do you have in your internship?"

She shied away, looking even more like a frightened puppy. "I'd love to stay and chat, but I'm running very late."

"I realize that. You might mention my concern to Mr. Chapman. I'm sorry, maybe another time." He stepped back and crossed his arms over his chest.

She smiled politely. "Enjoy the fireworks, Mr. Wright." Nikki turned to Jared and

Sandra, thanking them before making a quick escape.

Jared punched him playfully on the shoulder. "What are you thinking, man? She's an intern. She has no pull with old man Chapman."

He watched Nikki climb into an older-model sedan and shook his head. He had to admit, she didn't look or act like the typical money-hungry dates Jared usually set him up with, and he couldn't imagine anyone hiring such a meek woman as a reporter for the city's largest newspaper. Still, there was something intriguing about Nikki Post. "I wouldn't bet on that one."

Nikki took a deep breath and closed herself inside the compact car. What a mess. She felt her face flush just thinking about what Colin must think of her after seeing the tantrum she had thrown over the car breaking down. She'd been dressed in her worst sweats, hiding under a baseball cap and just getting over the flu the day she'd hidden from him at the gym. How could he have even recognized her? Now this.

What an impression I must have made. After his comments about rich girls with no hearts, she wished they'd never met. It was far easier to admire his lean athletic build, drop-dead smile and well-groomed appearance without the tainted memories.

The shower had been the perfect opportunity to let the tears flow. The accident had sent her back to spring semester of her freshman year of college when she'd overheard her dance instructors. *Nicole is nothing more than a spoiled, chubby wannabe. Someone should have had the courage to tell her she had no future in dancing long ago.*

The incident had been the start of a dark time in her life that she'd tried to forget. She had literally stopped eating, begun exercising, lost more than she had gained since arriving at school and danced even harder to prove them wrong. The final blow came during the audition for an exclusive dance troupe. Torn ligaments and extensive surgeries ended her dream of a professional dancing career.

The injury gave Nikki's advisor the necessary ammunition to force her to drop her dance major. Friends encouraged her to find another aspect of performance until the injury healed, but she couldn't carry a tune and she had no acting talent. She had taken the semester off and sunk into her own self-pity.

She looked over her shoulder, to the

shadows of Colin and Jared next to the house with the fireworks behind them. She had recognized Colin's magnetic smile immediately and tried to leave. Suddenly she felt angry and confused, just as she had on the day her dreams were ripped out from under her.

Nikki's hand automatically turned the key in the ignition and then turned on the radio as she pulled away from the party. "Just find another dream," she whispered, wishing she could fend off her skepticism. "How difficult can that be?" She got onto the interstate, barely noticing the fireworks. Her mind wandered back to the doubt she'd seen in Colin's eyes. She should be used to that look by now. She'd grown up with it.

Again, a year later, after her third surgery, her parents had encouraged her to take time off from school to evaluate her future. She'd quickly figured out that they expected her to find a wealthy husband and give up on finishing her degree. And they'd almost succeeded, with Rory Drake's help.

The pressure from their breakup, school and her parents' disapproval had sent her further into a depression. She'd gained back every ounce she'd lost, plus some by graduation. When her grandfather had invited her to become an intern at the newspaper to see if she would like to follow in his footsteps she'd accepted the challenge. For a while she had thought she'd found something to make her parents proud of her. Apparently this wasn't the right decision either. One day in the copyeditor's seat and she had people angry with her already.

She might have an eye for writing, but she obviously had no savvy when it came to journalism. She'd had to fill in with that article for this morning's paper. If she hadn't had to cover for the copyeditor in a pinch, this would never have happened.

She quickly walked the two blocks from the parking lot carrying a fruit tray for the Labor Day potluck the staff had planned. Morale needed a boost, according to the managing editor. Which, of course, meant eating.

Everyone had brought treats, yet she felt more than conspicuous adding her contribution to the table after everyone had already served themselves. Thinking of all the delicious calories on the huge table, she pushed her way through. "Here's a fruit tray, help yourself." For the first six months of her internship, she'd gained steadily, despite her efforts to go to the gym. Only recently had she broken through and started losing. She wasn't about to blow it now.

Quietly, Nikki fixed a plate, then headed back to her desk. She sat down and began to contemplate the direction her life was going.

Misty turned her chair around to face Nikki's. "Surely your diet can have a day off!"

She glanced at her friend, mustering a quick smile. "Oh, it's had a day off already. I just came from a picnic," Nikki said softly. "I found out that I made a big mistake last night with some filler I used in place of the water-theft article. Apparently some people think we should ignore both sides of the shelter issue."

Misty nodded. "I've heard this issue is getting heated. So what?"

She nodded and silently turned back to her computer. Nikki had been surprised to find she enjoyed the fast pace of the newspaper. She hadn't minded any aspect of the job, until today. She hoped the copyeditor would be back at work tonight so Nikki couldn't make any more mistakes. How had she let her grandfather talk her into this?

"Is something wrong?" Misty rolled her chair closer. Misty looked into her reddened eyes and must have seen more than barbecue sauce. "It is, tell me what's happened."

"I met the man doing the fund-raiser for the homeless shelter at the picnic tonight. He wasn't very happy with our support of the other side."

"What support?"

"Remember, I filled in for Michelle last night? We were short on copy, so I took this one from the top of the list." She picked up the paper on her desk, turned to the article and waited while Misty read it.

Finally, Misty said, "This is a newspaper, not a periodical. Journalism is putting your own beliefs aside to tell the full story. That piece was not an editorial. Colin isn't used to someone opposing his causes. That story told about the reasons the opposition is fighting the shelter going into their neighborhood. You didn't do anything wrong. News is what sells papers. Is that what has you so blue tonight? He's in the business. He should know that conflict is what sells papers."

Nikki thought again of Colin Wright. Of his big smile, and those deep blue eyes that seemed to reach to the depths of her soul. How could she explain her mangled emotions to anyone without seeming like a spoiled rich girl?

Don't do something stupid, Nikki. She'd had these low days before, and they always seemed to pass. “Yeah, I guess you’re right. I thought I was going to be in trouble.”

“Nah! You’re going to have to get a thicker skin if you’re going to survive in this business, kid.”

Nikki laughed. Misty couldn’t be any more than five years older than she was. “Kid?”

Misty blushed. “Sounded good to remind myself that I’m not the new kid on the block anymore. You’re not the first to have a tough time with the requirements of the job. We all go through it time and again. Some days it’s really tough to be a good employee and a Christian when it’s obvious that some journalists live for sensationalism. That’s probably what Colin wanted to think.”

Nikki looked at her friend’s bright face and returned the sympathetic smile. “Thanks, Misty. I feel like there’s just so much I don’t know about publishing.” Misty had taken Nikki under her wing from Nikki’s first day on the job. Even she hadn’t made the connection between Nikki and her grandfather, which would make it even more embarrassing that Nikki knew so little about the industry when people started figuring it out. She made a mental note to enroll in some journalism classes at the college next semester. She had put it off too long already. With a degree in business administration with an emphasis in nonprofit organizations, she'd thought Grandfather would find a job that matched her skills. *Now I do sound like a spoiled rich girl.*

"Take a break, Nikki. You're way too hard on yourself. I don't know what burdens you're holding inside, but it's time you cast them aside. Life is too full of opportunities to dwell on what's already past."

That would be wonderful advice, if she only knew how.

"Nikki, in my office, please," the managing editor said as he walked past, a platter of food in front of him.

"Great, I told you I'd be in trouble."

Chapter Five

"Close the door," Paul said as Nikki stepped into his office.

So much for Misty's encouragement. Nikki had made a big mistake, and now they were going to fire her. Even her grandfather couldn't rescue her now.

"I understand Colin Wright called in and complained about the article on the home owners' fight against the sale of the lot in their neighborhood."

She nodded, wondering if he'd overheard her telling Misty about it, or if Colin had talked to Paul himself.

"I want to assure you that you wouldn't have seen that story on the copyeditor's list if it hadn't been approved. Michelle is going to be out for a few more weeks and we think you're ready to move up."

"Really?"

Paul chuckled. "You can move your belongings into the desk behind Anne's for now."

"Now? Tonight?"

"Unless you have something better to do, Anne will start training you tonight."

Nikki stood and sidestepped to the door. "Of course not. Thank you."

She hurried to tell Misty, who smiled with that all-knowing attitude of hers. "Told you so. Before you know it you'll be looking down from the corner office."

She laughed nervously. "Hey, maybe I can jump right over the reporter stage of the internship."

"Now you *are* dreaming," Misty said, tossing her empty plate into the trash. "Enjoy the new job. I'll miss your company."

Nikki found a box and moved the contents of her desk to the new one down the hall. She and Anne worked closely for a few hours, then she settled into the layout for the next night's feature stories. Within the week, Nikki was working independently on the earlier shift.

Four days later she was called to the managing editor's office again. What could she have done this time?

She folded her hands in her lap and waited, glancing over her shoulder now and again. She caught a glimpse of Paul as he barreled toward his office, around the maze of desks. He took a deep breath, seated himself behind his desk and shuffled through the papers piled on top without saying a word. He pulled one from the stack and handed it to Nikki. "This explains the assignment far better than I could," he said gruffly.

"Assignment?" That was a term normally reserved for the reporters, not editors.

He shrugged. "I had nothing to do with the decision. Read it for yourself."

She read the memo with her name at the top and Grandfather's signature at the bottom. Nikki's heartbeat doubled, her voice faded to nothing. "But . . . why?"

"Don't ask me. Apparently I'm just the messenger around here. Chapman took Amanda off the story and put you on. I guess today's your lucky day. You'll be working with Gary. He'll keep up on the fight for the land here while you're on the road. Meet with him in the morning to get started." The managing editor snatched a stack of papers from his basket and stormed out of the door. "The way I understand it, you have a week until your new assignment, so let's put tonight's issue to bed before you get too excited."

Excited was an overstatement. *Terrified* was more like it.

On her way back to her desk she avoided the temptation to look up at Grandfather Chapman's office window, overlooking the cluttered desks below.

Everyone knew her simply as Nikki Post, intern and aspiring journalist. She had hoped the internship would be short-lived and she could jump right into the management office, which suited her personality far more. The business manager was long past retirement and Nikki was getting impatient waiting to move into the junior ranks for his position.

Yet while she wanted the business office job, she wanted to earn it on her own merits, not because she was the owner's heir. That was the agreement, and if Grandfather felt she needed the internship to prepare her for the business world, she would trust him. But trusting him didn't mean she would enjoy every step along the way.

During the past ten months she'd learned almost every aspect of the newspaper except one. Reporting. Even she hadn't a clue why her grandfather had put her into this miserable situation. She stared at the assignment in disbelief.

Two weeks with Colin Wright, the man who had reached celebrity status more from raising money for charitable causes than because of his baseball career. Ironically, Colin was all she'd heard about on the news, the radio, and at work since the picnic at Jared and Sandra's. She just wanted the fund-raiser to be over. Double that sentiment now. She thought she had figured out a guaranteed way to avoid him at the gym by going late in the afternoon when his talk show aired, but even that hadn't worked. His voice met her at the gym door, as they played his show over the speaker system. Now it seemed her efforts were for naught.

Gary tossed his clipboard onto the stack of messages on his desk, sending loose papers flying. "Evening."

She jumped. "Hi," she all but whispered.

"I hear you've reached the pinnacle of your newspaper career." Gary glanced at the mock-up for the next day's paper and added it to the stack. "Congratulations. What's the scoop?"

She didn't dare tell the best reporter on Grandfather's staff that she'd never written a publishable article in her entire life. Nor did she have any desire to do so now. Nikki wasn't a journalist. She liked working behind the scenes — way behind the scenes. One day soon her grandfather would realize his mistake. Very soon. She looked down, wishing she had someone she could confide in. "You don't know?"

He laughed. "Well, I understand we're going to work together. Are you okay with that?" She nodded half-heartedly. Gary leaned against the desk and laughed at her answer. "Can't be that bad, it'll get you out of copyediting."

Nikki liked copyediting. She'd even come to enjoy writing headlines. "I suppose that's one way to look at it. I'm just not so sure I'm really ready for reporting."

"I haven't found the memo yet, what's our assignment?"

Nikki cringed. "Some radio jock thinks he can make it from New Mexico to the Wyoming border in a week — no, that's when we start . . ." she glanced at the memo again, noting the handwritten scribbles ". . . make that eight days for his relay deadline."

"I heard rumblings of his latest stunt. Colin Wright, from WWJD radio, right?" Gary patted her shoulder and laughed. "Talk about a cushy first assignment. You'll have some luxury motor home to travel in and the exclusive story that everyone and his dog will be following. The whole city could burn down and no one would care, but get Colin on the fund-raising committee, and the city stands at attention." Gary went on, appearing to be irritated, yet impressed at the same time by the attention Colin received. "If any of the rest of us went down the Sixteenth Street Mall pushing a peanut with our nose, we'd be sent to the loony bin. He does it, and out come the TV crews and pocketbooks," he said with a contagious laugh.

"So I've heard. Seems a little juvenile to me."

"Just young at heart. Colin's a good guy. The boss must like you."

She shrugged uncomfortably. "Funny, I was wondering what I'd done to tick him off." She couldn't wait to find out exactly what Grandfather was thinking. They'd agreed that she wouldn't be expected to write. She'd rather be running the business, not ruining it.

Unfortunately, her questions would have to wait until she got home, where there was no chance of anyone eavesdropping on their conversation. "Have a good day, Gary. I'm not on the beat till tomorrow. What time should I report?"

"Is eight too early?"

"Actually, I'm still on copyediting tonight. Could we make it eleven?"

"Sure, that'll work fine. And don't worry about this assignment, what could go wrong?"

Nikki returned to her desk and tried to regain her focus on the fourth page in the Faith section of the Friday paper, where the feature article was Colin and the fund-raiser. She just couldn't seem to get away from him.

Little did Gary know how much could go wrong when it came to Nikki's writing. Not that she didn't like writing, but all she knew about the journalistic format was what she had learned from proofreading and copy-editing.

Paul barked orders across the room and Nikki had no more trouble focusing on her current job. There were several aspects of her present life that she wouldn't miss. Working when most everyone else was at home sleeping was one. Daily breakdowns of the presses wouldn't be missed, either. Barking, overstressed editors would definitely be third on the list.

At the end of her shift, Nikki slung the straps of her leather handbag over her shoulder and prepared to leave. She sensed Grandfather watching as she stepped into the dark morning, which was ridiculous; he was probably at home sound asleep right now.

"Good night, Miss Post," the security officer said. "Would you like me to walk you to your car?"

Nikki forced a smile and shook her head. "Thanks, Wes, I'll be careful." Walking down the street to the economy lot, she was especially mindful of the corners that had become shelters for the homeless. When she reached the car she peered into the backseat, then looked around before inserting the key into the lock.

Nikki felt a chill on her neck, as if someone was watching her. She looked around as she tried to turn the key, but couldn't see anyone. She jiggled the key every which way until it finally moved. She threw her purse and the memo into the passenger seat and scooted inside. Nikki slammed the door and locked it, vowing to buy a new car, with or without family money. Surely a reporter's salary would allow her to get something more reliable than this.

When Grandmother had suggested she move to Denver after college, it was a perfect opportunity to avoid facing her parents' disappointment. Until the day she had overheard her dance instructors talking, she hadn't realized how pampered she had been growing up.

Her parents had encouraged and admired her every move, never accepting the fact that she wasn't destined for greatness. She thrived on their praise, blinded by their vision for her. They were furious when she broke her engagement to Rory and went into denial when she had to give up dancing. Only then did she realize her problem wasn't a lack of talent, but that she simply hadn't found the right one yet.

Her grandparents had been the only ones who understood Nikki's need to find her own way. She wanted to be loved for herself — not for her connections or her parents' money.

Grandmother had been the one to suggest that Nikki not mention her family or their status in the community until she was ready to do so. It had worked so far. She hadn't told a soul and she was feeling good about her friendships.

Still, when Grandfather had shown her this car, insisting that she didn't want to draw attention to herself, she'd wanted to cry. There had to be a happy medium between this heap of junk and the collector-series convertible her parents had given her for her college graduation.

Thankfully, Grandmother had put her foot down when it came time to find Nikki an apartment. She found a small but comfortable condominium in a newer area that wouldn't raise too many suspicions.

Nikki bit her lower lip and worried it between her teeth. As friendships grew stronger, she felt more uncomfortable holding back her identity, as if she should be ashamed of her family. If Colin's opinion counted, maybe she should be.

The assignment rolled around in her mind, leading to more questions. Did Grandfather want her to go with Colin because she was family? Did he not trust Colin? And if so, what was her complete role in this? Watchdog? Relay police? Enforcer? She didn't like the prospects at all. Colin Wright didn't appear to be the type to want a woman telling him what he could and couldn't do.

Grandfather didn't know anything about the mishap at the barbecue, the flowers and card that Colin had sent the following week as an apology for ruining her clothes, or her struggle to forget the man.

How could she tell Grandfather that while she appreciated his encouragement she did not want this assignment? She might not know exactly what she did want to do with her life yet, but she didn't need any hands-on experience to know that she wasn't cut out to be a reporter. Had coming to work here been a mistake after all?

The many nicknames she'd heard for Grandfather over the last ten months came back to her. She'd seen enough to understand why some employees were unhappy with him. He had many decisions to make each day, and some, like assigning her to Colin Wright's story, were without a doubt going to make someone unhappy. She sympathized wholeheartedly.

When she got home, her answering machine was flashing. Knowing it was probably her grandfather trying to reach her, she touched the play button and began changing into a tank top and cotton boxers then stretched out across the bed to rest before her morning run. Good thing today was a ten-miler. She needed it.

"Nicole, meet me at the house for breakfast in the morning. I want to explain this assignment to you." The machine beeped to signify the end of her messages and Nikki drifted off to sleep.

When she awoke from her nap, she changed clothes, tied her running shoes and took off for her grandparents' house. Eight miles later she entered the code into the security system and passed through the tall wrought-iron gate as it opened.

Grandfather met her at the door. "I don't like you running at this time of day by yourself, Nicole. You never know who could be watching you."

She lifted her right hand to reveal a can of

Mace, and a cell phone dangling from the left one. "I'm careful." Nikki leaned forward to give him a kiss, wondering if he had seen someone hanging out at the newspaper recently. Don't be ridiculous, Nik, it's just your imagination, she thought. "I was shocked by your memo. I thought we agreed I'd somehow skip over the reporter phase of the internship."

He patted her shoulder. "Not even any small talk this morning?" He nodded. "I know you don't want to write, but I need you on this assignment, Nicole."

She opened a bottle of spring water and poured it over ice in a crystal goblet. "I wouldn't know where to start to write an article for a newspaper. Especially for one the size of the *Gazette*."

Grandfather looked at her with such astonishment that she was ashamed of herself for disagreeing with him. "I trust you, Nicole. You won't let me down."

"I simply don't want to embarrass you, Grandfather. I know there's a lot riding on Colin finishing the stunt, and I've never written anything for publication."

Grandmother joined them then, carrying a platter of fresh fruit. "Morning, Nicole. This is quite a treat to have you here for breakfast today."

Nikki followed Grandmother to the kitchen to help serve the rest of the meal. "It came as quite a surprise to me as well, but at least a nice one. You do know what's happened, don't you? Grandfather has assigned me to write articles on Colin Wright's fundraiser!"

Grandmother handed Nikki a homemade quiche and followed with a basket of pastries and a pitcher of juice. "You'll do just fine, darling. Sometimes it's good to stretch ourselves."

"Is that what you call this? Stretching myself? Humph." Nikki set the pie plate onto the trivet and seated herself between her grandparents. Grandmother said a quick blessing, barely squeezing it in before Grandfather continued to discuss her assignment.

"I'm not kidding when I say I have no clue how to write an article, Grandfather."

"You read the newspaper every day. You're a bright girl . . ." Every insecurity from her childhood returned with that one phrase, *bright girl*. She'd heard it often enough from her teachers, her dance instructors and even her parents. It had turned out to mean she wasn't the most intelligent girl in the class, nor the most talented dancer, and she'd better find another means of support. She nibbled on her quiche and bypassed the temptation to drown her sorrows with a Danish.

"Nikki, are you listening to me?" Her grandfather's gruff voice shattered the dismal visit to her childhood. "If you'd feel better, I'll arrange for a crash course on interviewing and reporting, but Gary is a perfect mentor. He will make sure your stuff is ready for the paper. I'm sure with a couple of practice pieces, you'll be up to speed in time for the race."

"Race? What race?" She swallowed the lump of crust, wondering what she had missed. "Who is he racing against?"

"Race, fund-raiser, relay: whatever you want to call it. Colin is racing against time and especially the opposition to the project. I need you there."

Nikki set her napkin on the table and looked at her grandfather. "Why *me?* You have dozens of great reporters who could do much more for this article."

"There's a lot riding on this event, Nicole." Grandfather explained that he'd been contacted by an investment group, hoping to sway the newspaper's support for the shelter. Home owners in the area didn't want a shelter to bring down the value of their homes and investors had supposedly been trying to negotiate a deal on the land for an office building. "People will be buying newspapers just to see if Colin can pull this one off. We have exclusive coverage, which means there will be limited access to all other news agencies, including television. I want to work every mile out of this story. He's trying to raise half a million dollars, and there are plenty of people who'd love for him not to succeed."

Nikki shook her head. "I still don't understand why one or the other can't find a different property and let everyone win on this issue."

Grandfather chuckled. "If only life were so easy . . ."

She glanced from her grandfather to her grandmother and back again, reasoning through the information. "And why is it so important to you that I personally cover this story?" She took a drink of fresh-squeezed orange juice.

"I don't trust just anyone with this issue. The investors are upset with my involvement, your parents and aunts and uncles think I've lost my mind, and yet, I know it's the very best investment I could make for the community. Besides, you're our only reporter who is physically up to the challenge, and I want someone with Colin at all times."

The acidity of the juice caught a dry spot on her throat and sent her into a coughing spell. A few minutes later, when she'd recovered, Nikki challenged her grandfather even further. "I'm going to *do* this stunt *with* him?" The thought of eight days, twenty-four hours a day with that man made her stomach turn. "Surely there's someone on staff that you trust."

Her grandfather hesitantly shook his head. "That's not the point, Nicole. It's your future on the line."

Nikki knew instantly that this had little to do with covering a story or even the success of the project. She looked at the fine china plate and crystal goblets with regret and shame. "I think I understand why you want me there."

He took her hand. "I want to be sure this goes well, Nicole. A vital part of the newspaper's success stems from our commitment to this community. It's been good to our family. More important to us is our moral obligation to give back. The Bible says, 'Judge not that we be not judged, be merciful because the Father is merciful to us, give that it shall be given unto you.' God has been more than merciful to our family, Nicole, and it's my prayer that each of you will learn the importance of giving back to those less fortunate."

Nicole nodded, slightly confused about why her grandfather was preaching the gospel to her all of a sudden. He and Grandmother had wanted her to go to church services with them, but realized the closer they were, the harder it would be for Nikki to make her own mark on the world. "Are you feeling okay, Grandfather?"

He looked at her in shock. "I'm fine, Nikki. There are just a few more things I've been wanting to tell you. You're almost through with the internship, and George has been talking about his retirement."

Nikki felt her heart beating against her ribs. She couldn't believe Grandfather was actually ready to give her the chance she'd been wanting.

"I've been praying since you were a young girl that the Lord would convince you of your need for salvation." He shook his head. "Nothing has been more difficult than watching my children drift in and out of a walk with the Holy Spirit, and not guiding you kids to the Lord, either. I want you to know that I try my best to run this newspaper with Christian values and morals. Though not everyone on my staff understands or knows that, I pray every night that His word will change their lives." Grandfather took a deep breath and let it out. "I saw a change in you the night you walked away from marrying Rory and I think you know how proud that made your grandmother and me to see you stand up for yourself. But there's more we want for you than watching out for yourself. I want you to watch out for others, as well. The homeless situation is a perfect example. It's not just drunks who sleep on the park benches. There are families torn apart because they can't find shelters that have room for all of them. Kids who are abandoned because parents hope they'll have a better chance of finding a good home. One shelter won't solve all of the problems, but it is a start."

Nikki stole a glance at her grandmother, whom she'd never seen so quiet. The tears in Grandmother's eyes were contagious. If this was so important to them, she wouldn't argue. "Okay then, what do I do now?"

"Colin knows just what to expect from reporters. He doesn't open up to them anymore."

"And you think I can . . ."

"I do. I think there's something deeper than commitment to his job motivating him. You saw the change in him when he heard it was for the homeless. I want someone who can get under his skin to the truth about what makes a man go to such lengths for strangers. That's the real story. And I want you to get it."

Chapter Six

Later that morning Gary showed her how to pull information from previous news stories from the archives. She had spent hours reading articles that made Colin Wright sound like an immature, egotistical, overgrown boy who couldn't turn down a dare. And from his comment at the picnic, Nikki had to admit she had plenty of her own questions about his motives.

After her meeting with Gary, Nikki made arrangements to meet Colin. She stepped into Good Sam's Shelter, the renovated old schoolhouse that they wanted to replace, uncertain of what to expect. The large old windows welcomed the heat of the summer inside where fifteen or more sweaty people fanned themselves. The swamp cooler, though it was cheaper than AC, seemed to pump more moisture than cool air into the crowded space.

She looked at her watch, feeling as out of place as she had on the day she'd walked into the *Denver Gazette.* Ignoring beggars had become a necessary survival skill for her walk between the parking lot and the newspaper each night. She'd learned to keep moving and not look into their eyes. Grandfather had hired security officers to keep the route as safe as possible, but a few occasionally slipped past the patrols.

This was another side of the issue . . . the families. The part Grandfather wanted her to see. She'd also seen a side of her grandparents that she'd never known before, and she was beginning to understand where his longing for something more meaningful in her life came from.

In the next room, a rosy-cheeked baby wailed as his obviously exhausted mother tried to coax him into taking a bottle. Another teary-eyed child tugged at the mother's leg. "Mama . . ." she whined.

Around the corner, the director shook her head, telling a young family that there were no more openings in the shelter. Nikki didn't need to understand Spanish to feel the couple's desperation.

Her lower lip worked its way between her teeth, and her heart squeezed tight. The mother shook her head, her eyes wide as she repeated, *"Comida."* She wanted food for her children. Nikki looked away, remembering Gary's advice: "Don't let your feelings for the subject get in the way of the story. You have to stay impartial."

How could she do that? She didn't know what circumstances had brought this young family to a shelter for help. She simply saw parents humbled and burdened and desperate. Nikki turned her attention back to the family next to her.

Looking around for something to distract the little girl and allow the mother to feed the baby, Nikki started building a cabin from a pile of toy logs. Silence filled the room. She looked at the mother. "Would your daughter like to play?" It only took a slight nudge of encouragement from the mom before Nikki had the child seated on her lap. Nikki helped the little girl match the notches on the logs.

"Me house?" the curly-haired toddler asked innocently.

Nikki felt her heart swell, then break at the thought of this family living on the streets. "Pretty, isn't it? What's your name?"

Dishes clanged in the kitchen and volunteers set rows of tables for the upcoming meal.

"Zasmin." The little girl with the brown eyes handed Nikki another log.

"It would be fun to live in a log cabin, wouldn't it . . . Jasmine?" Nikki hoped she'd deciphered the child's name correctly.

Jasmine nodded.

"Nicole Post. So you're the reporter assigned to this story. Interesting," the easily recognizable voice said matter-of-factly. She had listened to Colin's show that afternoon, resigning herself to the fact that she wasn't going to talk her grandfather out of having her cover this story. Why it had to be her, she still didn't totally understand, but she couldn't let him down. It made no sense that Colin Wright, a Christian disk jockey, would take advantage of her grandfather, but Grandfather had his reasons for wanting her here, whether she understood or not.

She looked over Jasmine's blond curls to the man standing beside them. "Fancy meeting you here." She felt her skin warm with the recollection of their previous meetings. "Pardon me for not getting up."

Colin knelt next to the toddler-size table. "Hi," he said to the little girl, flashing his warm smile. "What's your name?" Either Jasmine didn't hear Colin or she chose to ignore his question.

"This is Jasmine," Nikki said quietly. His denim-blue eyes glanced at the little girl and then up to Nikki, catching her off guard.

"Are you having fun today, Jasmine?"

"Yep. See me new house?" She jumped to the floor and rushed to Colin.

He welcomed her without hesitation.

"That's a really nice one, isn't it? I always wanted a log house, but I never got one."

Jasmine put another log on the growing pile, then placed a log in Colin's hand.

"Jazzy," her mother said, "it's time for us to get washed for dinner. Thank you, ma'am, for keeping her busy while I fed the baby."

Colin helped Jasmine to her feet and stood visiting with the mother. Connecting immediately, he offered to talk to her husband about a job interview. His compassion left a lump in her throat.

Nikki watched in awe, then fingered Jasmine's curls. "Thank you for building the cabin with me, Jasmine. Enjoy your supper, okay?"

The director of the shelter approached them. She introduced herself to Colin and invited them to eat dinner with them. "One of our families has parent conferences at the preschool tonight, so the volunteers prepared way too much food."

"Thanks, Kathleen." He turned to Nikki and waited.

Nikki could use all the distractions available, but she hesitated. "What about the family you had to turn away, couldn't they eat my meal?" Nikki asked.

Colin looked at her with that magnetic

smile. "Mine, too. We'll get something else."

"You two will make quite a team." The director smiled. "But it's not necessary for you to go elsewhere. They're completing the forms for our resident waiting list, but they will have supper with us. There really is plenty of food for everyone tonight."

"That would be nice. Thank you, Kathleen." The last thing Nikki wanted was to be one-on-one with one of the most popular radio personalities in town. Even those who didn't listen to Christian radio knew Colin Wright. "So, where do we start?"

"We can start by relaxing. We're going to be in much too close quarters to start out this assignment stepping on each other's toes."

A dimple softened his stubble-framed smile. She hadn't the time to notice him at the barbecue, and had avoided looking at him at the board meeting. He even had a nicely shaped head for the nearly shaved look. She forced a nod of agreement. This wasn't a good way to start, with her staring at the subject she was supposed to interview objectively.

Sitting with the director allowed Nikki the chance to glean a better understanding of the many facets of homeless families without asking one question. Nuclear-family lines were more difficult to determine once everyone was seated. Parents and older children helped the younger ones get served, seeming to know what each one liked and didn't like.

"Are the families at that table related?" Nikki whispered to Kathleen.

"Only by way of sharing this roof. Both families have been here for almost two months, so they've grown pretty close. Since many of the available jobs are during the late night shift, they have worked out a sort of child-care swapping arrangement. That's not the norm, however."

Colin asked about counseling for the families who participated in the program. "Are sessions required?"

"We offer workshops every evening after supper, but with the different family needs and jobs, it's impossible to require attendance. Most will attend at least once a week if only for the social benefits."

"Do you notice a personality type that seems to cope with this situation better than others?"

Kathleen thought for a few minutes before answering. "I wouldn't want to make generalizations, but there are some warning signs to watch for, and for everyone's protection, we help find other facilities for those individuals."

Listening to Colin in person, Nikki was surprised to discover the quality of her ten-dollar radio. His voice was just as low and husky in person as over the wires.

Nikki took a bite of lasagna and sensed someone watching her. She glanced at Colin and their eyes met.

"You're about the quietest reporter I've ever met. How long have you been at the *Gazette*?"

Nikki managed to swallow the remainder of her food without choking and took a drink of iced tea. "Ten and a half months." She felt as if the bright sunshine had burned her cheeks, but that was impossible. She hadn't spent any measurable time outside for days, thanks to her cram sessions for Journalism 101. From the look of Colin's tan, she couldn't believe he had a desk job. "You and Kathleen have answered all of my questions so far."

"You're kidding."

She was never going to be able to pull this off. He was already doubting her. "No, I'm getting what I need." Mentally, she reviewed the five elements to include in an article. Who? An incredibly handsome radio host. What? A relay to raise money for those less fortunate. When? Eight very long days. Where? Front range of the Rocky Mountains. Why? That, she had yet to figure out.

And in this story, the most interesting element would be how he planned to get from start to finish. She'd gone to the radio Web site to learn more about Colin and his program. Though she would be the first to admit her grandfather was right, Colin knew exactly what he wanted revealed to the public and what he didn't; she also sensed she could get more out of him. "I'm getting the gist of the problem."

"Really. You don't want to know how many families are homeless? Or what the anticipated cost of a new shelter will be?"

"I've done my homework, but if it would make you feel better, you can tell me and I'll write it down." She pulled out a pad of paper and waited for him to recite the information.

"You know how many families are without homes?"

"No, I doubt anyone knows the true answer to that one, but of those looking for shelters, there are an estimated seven thousand needing shelter on any given night. Sixty-five percent of those are families, and over three thousand of those are children. With the recent decline in donations, protests from the neighbors, and legal issues, this plan for building a new shelter is at risk of falling through. It's our job to see that doesn't happen."

Colin gave a tight-lipped smile. "Point made."

The director smiled as she stood to clear the table. "If you do need any questions answered, Nikki, give us a call. I'll be glad to help in any way I can. You have my cell phone number?"

"Yes. Thank you, Kathleen. I'll be in touch." Jasmine, her mother, and the baby went upstairs to the dormitory-style bunk beds. Colin stacked some of the serving bowls and carried them into the small kitchen where residents were struggling not to trip over one another. Nikki took a tray of glasses to the sink, and the residents thanked her and Colin for their help before sending them away.

Kathleen cleaned off the tables. School-age children ran up and down, making an awful racket on the oak stairs. Voices bounced off the high ceilings. How anyone got any rest here was a miracle in itself.

Colin leaned close. "Looks like a quiet corner over there, shall we sit down?" While they moved, Nikki thought over the questions she had in mind for the first feature.

Though she and Gary were to team up on it, they had agreed that he would handle the property-fight angle, and she would focus on Colin and the fund-raising story.

After several futile attempts to hear one another he leaned in again. She could feel the warmth of his breath on her ear. "Since you seem to have a sense of why we're doing this, why don't we find someplace a little quieter so I can fill you in on the plans."

She closed her purse and put the strap over her shoulder, still considering what was causing the tingle in her stomach. Must be nerves, she decided. She'd completed her cram course in interviewing after meeting with Gary. The teacher had even helped her outline some questions to get started. So why couldn't she think of anything to ask Colin?

"There's a coffee shop down the street." He paused before walking toward the door.

Maybe she should be digging for a little more of who Colin Wright really was, instead of going for his reasons for doing this. Despite his feelings about being set up with any more of Sandra's "rich" girlfriends, Colin did have that boyish twinkle in his eye that said, "I love life." Nikki would guess anyone who'd done all the crazy stunts Colin had would have to be at least part daredevil. She stepped out into the blast-furnace heat and took a deep breath, following Colin like a lost puppy.

"Is that okay?"

She looked at him, startled. Her mind reeled, trying to recall what he'd asked. "Fine."

"Would you like to walk, or drive or . . . fly, maybe?"

Fly? What in the world had she missed? "I beg your pardon?"

Her reaction seemed to amuse him. "So you are listening. I thought I'd lost you for a minute there."

"I was beginning to think you had, too. What did you ask, again?"

Colin's eyebrows peaked over his almond-shaped eyes. "I asked if there is someplace you'd rather go?"

Nikki felt her cheeks turning pink. "The coffee shop is fine." Maybe she needed some caffeine to wake her up so she didn't miss Colin's next turn in the conversation. "We may as well walk, we'll be doing a lot of that, won't we?"

"Not as much as I had hoped, but we'll definitely be getting a workout. Are you sure you're ready?"

She considered telling Colin now that she wasn't as sure of her readiness as her grandfather seemed to be, but worried that he would back out of the agreement. She didn't want to be the one to ruin the project. "As ready as anyone on staff, I suppose."

The walk went quickly, despite the record-setting fall temperatures. Colin opened the door to the coffee shop for her, pleased to see that the gesture surprised her. It was clear that Nikki came into this assignment with a biased opinion of him. One he completely deserved. He had a lot of ground to make up for the remark she'd overheard at the barbecue. While he wasn't pleased to find he had offended the one person Ellis had chosen to cover the story, he couldn't quite say he was outraged by Nikki's involvement, either.

He would be interested to find out if Jared was somehow involved in Ellis's selection of reporters. He suddenly remembered Nikki's denial of any responsibility for the earlier story about the home owners' fight. "I thought you said you weren't a reporter."

Nikki tucked a long strand of bangs behind her ear, revealing a simple solitaire earring. "I wasn't, then. This is my first assignment. Part of my internship."

Colin stopped in his tracks, still wondering why Ellis would give a story with such high stakes to a novice?

"Before you say it, don't think you're the only one wondering why I've been assigned to your story. As nearly as I can tell, I'm the only one G—" She paused, snapping her fingers, as if that would make the name come to her mind.

"The managing editor?"

"No."

"Oh, Gary?"

She shook her head. "No, um, Mr. Chapman made this decision."

She continued to surprise him. "Really?" He stared at her now, struggling to talk himself out of thinking something totally unprofessional was going on here.

"Mr. Chapman told me I'm to ride, or walk with you every mile. None of the other reporters are up to the physical challenge."

"Yeah, I bet." He approached the counter and ordered a tall iced coffee. "And what do you want?"

"Raspberry iced tea, please. I'll pay for my own, thanks anyway." She reached into a tiny pouch that he supposed she called a purse and he knew she was telling the truth about one thing. No reporter he knew carried anything so useless.

He took hold of her hand with his while digging his wallet from his hip pocket with the other hand. "I'm taking care of it."

She gazed at him through narrowed eyes, apparently just as puzzled by him as he was by her. "I begged to get out of this, I'll have you know. I even considered telling Mr. Chapman about your prejudices regarding people with money."

"I deserve that. But it's not all people with money, just women who worship all that money can buy. It's hard enough to come by. And even then, as long as they're not after *my* money, I don't care how they manage their own funds."

Nikki's perfectly proportioned lips formed an O and her eyebrows lifted. She forked her fingers through her hair, pulling it from behind her ear and letting it frame her face in smooth silken strands. Her chin lifted slightly, her shoulders stiffened, and her eyebrows arched, showing off incredibly beautiful eyes. "A little bitter, huh?"

Colin watched the subtle transformation with suspicion. So, maybe the earrings weren't fake. He nodded. "With good reason, so don't think that I'm totally biased to money. Depends on what a person does with what God gives them. There are plenty of people, such as Mr. Chapman, who give generously to the community. I'm sure God approves."

"And if they don't . . . you want nothing

to do with them? Maybe they have good reason for not giving."

Maybe he was getting himself into more trouble than he'd previously thought. It was sounding more and more as if Nicole Post fit into the same category as most of the women Jared and Sandra had set him up with. "It's the taking that's the main problem. That and priorities. And it's a rather private issue, so can we agree that I have no beef with wealthy people, in general?"

She took her glass from the counter and made her way to one of the tiny tables across the room. "Agreed. I think it would be wise to get back to the subject of the fund-raiser and stay there. I hope you don't plan to make coffee your beverage of choice on this excursion. I'm sure you're aware that it dehydrates you."

He saw no contempt in her expression and tried to keep from being annoyed. It was bad enough to have a novice journalist keeping tabs on him, but he didn't need someone bossing him around, too. "I'll keep it to a minimum. With stepping up my training regime and a double shift at the station tonight, a strong dose of caffeine is a definite must. I'm going to need to leave in an hour or so."

"Good thing I don't have many questions then, isn't it?" She opened her notepad and flipped to a page with impeccable printing on it.

"I thought you had all your answers already?"

"Then why did you suggest we come here?" She paused, and he refused to admit it was at least partially curiosity on a personal level. She didn't wait for an answer, but met his hesitancy with a confident smile. "Apparently you've been doing absurd stunts for quite some time now. How did you come up with some of your ideas?"

He hadn't considered the answer to that question in a good decade or more, and it would be unwise to divulge the entire story to a journalist who probably wouldn't connect with his journey of faith. "There isn't enough time tonight to go into the full explanation, but to some degree, it started as a dare."

She dropped her pen and stared at him, wide-eyed.

"Did I say something wrong?" He bent down to retrieve the pen the same time she did and they cracked heads.

"Ouch!" she said as she raised her head, hitting his temple with the force of a wild pitch. "No. It's just that your comment caught me off guard. Are you okay?" Nikki backed her chair farther away and stood as he rubbed his head in silence. "Let me get you some ice."

He didn't argue. Last thing he needed right now was a black eye. He watched her return from the counter with a small bag of crushed ice. She wrapped a couple of napkins around it and offered it to him.

"Thanks," he said, pressing the cold pack to his head. "So why'd my comment catch you off guard?"

Nikki's creamy complexion turned a deep peach. "I made a few judgments of my own, I guess. Based upon more stereotypes."

Stereotypes? Judgments of her own. So she felt he had made judgments about her, which must mean Nikki *was* from a wealthy family, or it wouldn't have upset her. He glanced at her black jeans and sweater, pondering her wardrobe more than he should. "You based your opinion of me on the fact that I accepted a dare?" He could only imagine what she'd think if he told her the full story.

Nikki took a long drink, though he didn't see a sign that the liquid was going down her throat. Finally she put the glass down and it was nearly as full as before. "I think we should start over, without any stereotypes and innuendos."

"Fine," he said coolly. "Colin Wright. It's nice to meet you."

"You, too. I'm Nikki Post."

He set the ice on the table and held out his hand to her. "I hear you're the new kid at the newspaper. I'm flattered to work with you." Her eyes twinkled, and Colin hoped she was quick to forgive.

Nikki's laugh was soft and cordial, but what caught him off guard was when she blushed. They were making progress. She took his hand and shook it. "It's rather intimidating to try to do justice to the notorious stunts of your past. I mean, you've done some pretty odd things, and raised an impressive amount of money for others."

"That was the fun part."

He wasn't sure what to read into the odd look she gave him. Admiration? Awe? Absolute contempt? Nikki took a deep breath and shook her head. "I feel like this is my first story ever, so I may need some writing advice from a pro."

"Not sure you've come to the right man. It's been a long time since I took journalism."

"So you planned a career in broadcasting?" She pulled her hand back and had her pen poised and ready.

Colin crossed his ankle over his other leg and leaned back in the chair. "No, actually, I planned to go into education. I always wanted to teach phys ed. When I started announcing the games while sitting the bench from a high-school soccer injury, I decided God had found a use for my big mouth and changed majors."

"What are your favorite sports?"

He thought a minute, realizing this was the reporter asking, not Nikki. "I don't have one favorite."

She looked up from her pad of notes, obviously annoyed. "You have to have a favorite."

He laughed. "It's kind of like asking your mom which kid is her favorite," he said. "No matter what she answers, it's going to hurt someone's feelings. Better we leave it that I love sports." They exchanged a few more surface questions and answers before Colin realized it was time to go.

She raised her fine, arched eyebrows in protest. "And I suppose you're going to leave me hanging on that?"

He looked at his watch. "In fact, I'm going to have to do just that. I barely have enough time to get to the station. Let me walk you to your car. It's not the kind of neighborhood to leave a lady alone."

"It's parked out front of the shelter. I'll be fine. I'd like to finish my notes. Go ahead."

He didn't think there was that much to write about, but that was her job. "We didn't get much time to talk about the relay. Here's my number at the station. Call me this evening and we'll set up a time to discuss more details."

Chapter Seven

Nikki put on an extra pair of thick socks and wrestled the clips of the brand-new Rollerblades closed.

Colin waited patiently. "I think that's a little tight. Why don't you try just one pair of socks."

She felt the blood backing up at her ankles and decided he was right. "Have you ever bladed before?" she asked. Why she hadn't thought to ask Colin more questions about that last night, she hadn't a clue. Now she was in for a cram session not only on journalism, but alternative transportation methods as well.

He nodded. "I'm on a roller-hockey team. Have you?"

"Never. I danced." She tugged the knee pads into place. "I feel like an invalid with all of the protective gear."

"If it keeps you from injury, it's worth it." He handed her the helmet. She could see immediately that the ponytail wasn't going to work with the helmet and tugged the band off. The elbow pads rubbed against her bare skin. She made a mental note to pack long-sleeved T-shirts to wear during the relay. She glanced at Colin, feeling like a child all bundled up for a blizzard. "Don't you have any knee and elbow pads?"

"I wear full gear during the hockey games, but don't expect to have any injuries today." Colin hesitated as he finished the sentence, as if remembering their continuous mishaps when they were together.

"So you do still participate in a sport?" Nikki said with a smile. "I guess that's what has you feeling pretty confident today. I look pretty wimpy compared to what you're used to. Maybe you should sign a waiver releasing me from responsibility if anyone gets hurt."

"You'll do just fine," he said, smiling. "This path is as smooth as it gets, and it doesn't have any large hills. I thought it would be a good beginner's route. What kind of dancing did you do?"

"Mostly ballet. I wanted to perform." She pushed herself off the park bench on her own, finding out very quickly that wheels on Rollerblades moved much more easily than old-fashioned roller skates did when she was a kid.

Colin offered his hand, and again she ignored his offer. "Really? What stopped you?"

Nikki ignored his question and his hand as she struggled to gain her balance.

"Easy. Here . . ." Colin cleared his throat, as if irritated with her stubborn independence. She was wearing knee pads, that would have to do for her protection. She didn't want to lean on Colin. Not while blading, during the relay, or any other time.

"I'm getting it," she said apprehensively, gliding forward. Colin jumped each time she wobbled, as if he were watching a toddler who was just learning to walk. She got the giggles just thinking of his nervous twitch.

"The key to learning to blade is to not make any sudden movements . . ." he warned.

Her skates kept moving faster and her arms went up and down like oars on a canoe. Colin glided ahead of her and spun ninety degrees, skating backward, advice rolling from his tongue, faster with every word. "Your brake is on the heel." The sidewalk curved and her arms flapped like propellers.

"Here, take my hands," he said as she spun out of control. He reached for her hands, his going up when hers went down.

She reached her hands in front of her, and he grabbed hold of them, steadying her as they slowed to a stop.

"I'm not doing this, I don't care what Gr . . . Mr. Chapman says."

Colin's hands tightened around hers, not allowing her to pull away. "You'll get the hang of it. Have you ever ice-skated?" His smile was disconcertingly compassionate.

She shook her head, and they both said, "No, I danced," at the same time, and she couldn't help but laugh.

"My dance instructor wouldn't let us take any extra risks. No skiing, no tennis or . . ." She realized she didn't need to elaborate. "Or any other sports for that matter."

"What?" His eyebrow arched high on his forehead. "Didn't she ever hear of cross-training?"

She laughed, suddenly nervous. "I guess not. I didn't start running until rehab after surgery to repair my anterior cruciate ligament. By then it was too late."

"It's never too late." He started moving slowly, fighting her to keep her hands closer to her sides. "When you lift one hand, it helps to turn your body the other direction, so when you want to go straight, you need to keep your arms close to your body and under control." He braked unexpectedly and she ran into him.

"Oh." Her running into him didn't faze

him a bit. She raised her chin, gazing into his eyes just long enough to realize that was a mistake. "Sorry. I didn't realize you were stopping." She got a close-up of the alluring way he trimmed his stubble to accentuate his strong jaw.

"I'll live. Balance a minute and watch me." Colin glided slowly and smoothly down the path, offering hints and suggestions every now and then, while she studied his every move. "Ready to try it again, or do you want a hand?"

The thought of his strong hand holding hers was too distracting. She wanted to do it on her own, if only to prove to him that she wasn't handed everything on a silver platter.

She knew what Colin thought of those more fortunate, and of those less. All of her life people had treated her differently when they found out her family had money. Only in the last few years she realized that most of the men in her life had cared more about how her family status could benefit them than they actually cared about her. She was tired of the letdown when she discovered their interest went only as deep as her pocketbook.

Even Colin was only here because of the relay and her grandfather's money. She couldn't confuse that with a personal interest in Nikki Post, the woman. "I'll try it myself, thanks."

"We're in this together, you know."

Of course, she thought, without her and Grandfather, Colin's project would be a failure. "Don't worry about me, I'll get up to speed on it. I do wish I'd had a little more notice to train for this." Despite the fact that Colin had no idea she and Ellis Chapman were related, she had a difficult time keeping her heart and her mind on separate tracks when it came to men. This was her first experiment with anonymity outside the office, and it already had its challenges.

While she was distracted with her own concerns, Colin took hold of her hand and set them into motion. They skated in silence for a few hundred feet before he let go of her hand. "I don't understand why Mr. Chapman insists you participate, especially with an old injury, or didn't you tell him about it?"

"Oh, he knows," she said without fully considering why an employer would know about an old injury. She paused a moment before continuing. "I even used that to try to convince him I'm not the right person for this job, but he's sponsored me on fund-raising walks, so my excuses fell on deaf ears. He gently reminded me that I can't have it both ways."

"See what I mean? Ellis is a generous man. Which other fund-raisers have you done?"

"The Race for a Cure and the MS Walk," she said hesitantly. "I just started doing them this year. It makes the benefits of walking that much more rewarding." Her grandfather had been her largest contributor for the multiple sclerosis and the fight against breast cancer, but she had also received pledges from co-workers and sorority sisters, as well. "So you see, there were several reasons he wouldn't let me out of this." Nikki was beginning to feel comfortable on the wheels and sped up.

"I'm glad he didn't," he said, and they exchanged a polite smile.

They bladed for half an hour before coming to a sizable hill. Nikki groaned. "This reminds me of muscles I haven't used since my dancing days."

"I remember I have them about once a week, after every game." He gave her tips to make the climb easier. "Our challenge on the relay will be rocks and gravel on the side of the road. If Mr. Chapman wouldn't mind, I'd suggest getting you a pair of street skates, too. They have wider wheels so you have a little more control."

"Maybe we should carry a broom, like

they use in . . ." she waved her hands as she tried to think of the sport ". . . you know, where they use the broom to clean the ice in front of the . . . Oh, what is it called?"

A couple bicycling toward them forced Colin to slow down and step behind her. "You mean curling?"

"Yes, that's it!" Nikki raised her hand in excitement and her feet failed to respond when she tried to regain her balance. Just before she anticipated hitting the hard cement, she felt Colin's strong hands grab under her arms and lift her into his embrace.

"Gotta watch those arms," he said firmly. She looked over her shoulder, surprised by the flash of anger in his eyes.

"I'm sorry," she said softly. "I guess my dance instructor was right to prohibit other athletic endeavors."

Nikki saw a photographer raise his camera toward them. Had Grandfather arranged for one of the staff photographers to follow them? She froze. Who else could have known where they were?

His hands dropped to her waist momentarily as she regained control. "I don't think that has anything to do with it. Blading just takes practice. You really are doing great for your first attempt. Most people fall immediately when they stand up that first time."

"Oh, so you teach a lot of skaters, huh?"

He spun around her, a mischievous look in his eyes. "Have to do something to keep myself out of trouble. I volunteer at the boys and girls club every week."

Nikki laughed, suddenly very aware that she was beginning to like the friendly banter between them. Too much. She didn't need another disappointment. Especially not with two more weeks together. That was just enough time to develop a really lethal crush on someone, and much too long to be able to avoid it. Especially when Colin Wright was the lethal weapon. "Are we almost back to the parking lot?"

Colin looked around. "We're about halfway. We can turn around or go on ahead. Are you okay?"

"I'm fine, just don't want to overdo it the first day. That and there's someone taking our picture," she said with a whisper. She started skating again, more careful to keep her arms close to her body.

"Yeah, I saw him follow you into the lot. I figured he was from the newspaper. It's one of the things you'll have to get used to. When you're in the public eye, people get curious about you."

"Yeah, I suppose so," she said cautiously.

"So what else do you do to keep busy? Do you run?"

"Not unless it's to get from one base to another."

"As in baseball, right?"

He laughed. "Right."

"Do you miss it?"

"I did right after my injury, but after that season ended, so did my drive for the action." Colin said it so casually she had to repeat it to herself to analyze it.

"You played professional ball?" How had she missed that in her research?

"It was a short career, but I don't miss it. Why, what kind of baseball did you think I played?"

Nikki laughed. "I'm not sure. I didn't really think about it until today, I guess. So I don't make any other mistakes, do you mind if I ask how you ended up in broadcasting?"

He took a few long strides then spun around and glided backwards. "Sports broadcasting positions were saved for retiring *successful* players, but I filled in for a few weeks after my surgery. When the season ended, I wasn't ready to find anything permanent. Mr. Chapman asked me to consider this job. I enjoyed radio and liked the idea of working where I could share God's promises."

"It seems sports announcing would have been a natural fit, too. Why'd you take this route?"

"I wanted a change and grew tired of the overblown attention on entertainment." He paused and whispered, "and sports." He spun around again and looked her in the eye. "That is off the record. I liked the idea of a more meaningful direction to my life. Even then it took more than a gentle nudge before I threw my hat into the race for the position."

To hear that all hadn't gone as planned for him boosted her image of him. Selfish of her, but still, it gave her hope that she could find the right direction one day.

By the time they reached the parking lot, Nikki felt a preview of the physical pain she would experience until the relay was over.

"How about tomorrow, same time?"

The adage "no pain, no gain" came to mind. With less than two weeks to prepare, she didn't dare take a day off. She would definitely make a trip to the hot tub in the clubhouse at her condo tonight. "What about cross-training?"

"Sure, what did you have in mind?"

"How about a bike ride or maybe a few laps in the pool to give these muscles a break?"

"No pool on the route, but the bike ride sounds good. Do you need a bike?"

She tugged the skates from her feet. "No, Mr. Chapman ordered one for me. Why don't we meet at the gym? We could take the path along the river."

"I have a better idea. It's my day off tomorrow. If you can afford the time, why don't we ride the mountain trail along I-70? That will give us a better aerobic workout and let us prepare for the higher elevation and mountain roads."

She peeled the thin sock from her foot, not surprised to find a half-dollar–size blister on her heel. "I'll do anything to stay off those skates for a few days."

Colin sat on the bench next to her and leaned over to look at her foot. "Ouch. Guess you might have wanted the thicker pair, after all."

She looked up and discovered his face was only about six inches from hers. Nikki pushed away the rising temptation to find out what kissing him would be like. "I've had plenty of experience with blisters. This is nothing a little moleskin and a thicker pair of socks won't remedy once it drains." It did mean the hot tub was out, though.

"Good," he said with an approving smile as he backed away and exchanged his own skates for shoes. “I like an athlete who isn’t afraid of a little pain.”

“Ditto.” Despite her attempts to avoid the situation, she had one problem — she was beginning to admire Colin a little too much. Comments like that one didn’t help. She tucked the wimpy socks into the blades and walked to her car barefoot, feeling at every step as if she were walking on hot coals.

Nikki decided right then to prove she was one competitor he wouldn’t soon forget.

Chapter Eight

Colin's mother insisted that even as a toddler, Colin could charm his way through any problem. He supposed that wasn't too far from the truth. After all, someone wise had also said there was a fine line between love and hate. Which he had a feeling was also true with Nikki Post. There was definitely tension between them.

They had ridden twenty-six miles along the Interstate-70 bike path, and stopped for lunch before heading back to Denver.

"So what do you do on the weekends?" Colin asked.

"Run my long-distance route, visit friends and family, do laundry, usual stuff. Of course, my weekend is usually Monday and Tuesday, so that makes it less interesting." She glanced briefly at him. There were no intimate gazes such as they'd shared yesterday.

"It does, doesn't it? Would you have time for . . ."

Nikki dug the key from her waist pack and knelt next to the bicycles. "That was a nice lunch, Colin. I'll have to remember this place if I come back."

He wasn't sure what she thought he was going to ask, but she either hadn't heard him or was afraid of hearing his question.

"So what do your weekends contain?" she asked. Nikki pulled her bike free from the rack and waited while Colin unlocked his.

"Sunday school and church. Mondays I run errands, then volunteer at the youth center." Here was his opening. "Do you worship?"

Her brows arched high above her ice-blue eyes. "You mean as in God? Do I go to church?"

He nodded at the same time as he answered. "Yeah."

"Occasionally," she finally answered. She glanced at her watch. "Wow, it's getting late. We'd better get going." She moved her helmet from her handlebars to her head and started riding.

Nikki apparently wanted nothing to do with mixing business and pleasure, as she was out of earshot within seconds. He had to admit, although he wasn't comfortable having a watchdog along, he was looking forward to getting to know Nikki better.

Colin considered asking her to join him at church, to get better acquainted with the driving force behind his life. If his one mention of God was any indication, it appeared she felt more than a little threatened by the subject.

Catching up with her, he decided to give conversation another attempt. "What's the rush? You have a hot date tonight?"

"If you consider working at the shelter hot, then yes, I do. I agreed to watch the kids while the parents attend the evening session."

"Really?" he said, stunned to silence. That was one project he wouldn't have expected her to enjoy, and it was the one he couldn't get involved with. He'd survived the one time meeting Nikki there, but he couldn't deal with the memories it brought back, from his dad's anger and broken pride at not being able to support their family to the taunting he and his sister had taken at school. He knew it was a worthy cause, and believed in the fund-raiser one hundred percent, but he couldn't get involved again. "Tell them hello for me."

"Do you volunteer there often?"

"No, shelters aren't one of my strengths, but a lot of the kids at the youth center come from shelters. The club is like an alternative to child care."

She looked at him with furrowed brow. "What's the difference?"

"Between what and what?"

"The shelters and the youth center? If they both have kids from shelters, what's the problem with helping at a shelter? It can't be that different, can it?"

He couldn't begin to explain. Not now. Not yet. Colin felt the same adrenaline rush that he'd felt the day they'd met and every time they were together. *Lord, when the time is right, help me to explain in a way that Nikki can understand and accept.* "Maybe not, maybe it's just my own issue."

They rode single file for half an hour without any conversation, then she sped up as if they were in the last mile of the Tour de France, leaving him to enjoy a few minutes of peace and quiet.

The majestic Rocky Mountains rose from the earth and touched the bright blue sky, reminding Colin that he wasn't in charge. God had already taken care of Nikki's faith issues, too, long before either of them were born. He sought comfort in the fact that someone else had taken care of the job of saving souls. It wasn't his job. Still, he longed to share the joys of God's grace with her.

On both sides of the bike path, wild grasses and flowers could almost make him forget that atop the hill were interstate highways that took travelers east and west to opposite ends of the state. Right now, that appeared to be how much distance Nikki preferred to keep between them, and sadly, it appeared that her faith was the main problem.

Again Colin questioned why Ellis had decided Nikki had to be the one to keep an eye on him. Colin decided it would be wise to give her some space to let her think about the seeds of faith that he'd planted.

Nikki had rounded the curve and disappeared from sight nearly fifteen minutes before. Since there were several curves ahead where he'd lose sight of her, he sped up to close the gap between them.

Had his simple mention of worship bothered her that much? He rounded the second curve and flew right past someone resting on the grass. He glanced back, realizing they hadn't met any other cyclists all day. He slowed down and looked ahead. Even though he'd sped up, there was no sign of Nikki. Could that have been her?

Colin turned around and went back to double-check. When he was finally close enough to recognize her, Nikki had curled into a ball, holding her knees to her stomach.

He jumped off the bike and let it fall to the

ground. "What happened?"

She looked up at him with apparent displeasure, as if he'd caused this. "I cramped up is all. I'll be fine."

He could remind her that she had taken the lead and was the one riding out of control, but he didn't. He got his water and handed it to her, then hesitated. "Stomach cramps or legs?"

"Charlie horse."

"You're sure it isn't anything more serious?"

She let out a breath and glared at him. "I'm sure. It's not even the same leg as my ACL surgery."

He handed her the water and asked which leg hurt the worst. As he waited for an answer, he examined her legs, noticing a light scar running from her knee clear down to the ankle of one leg. "How long ago was the injury?"

She shrugged. "Three or four years now, I guess. I'm not sure right now."

He gently pulled her legs straight even though she silently resisted. "Come on, you need to stretch it out. You know it as well as I do."

Her silent grimace proved to Colin that Nikki was as determined as he when it came to sports. Pain and cramps went with the territory. "Okay, I've got it," she said, her knees still bent at almost forty-five degrees.

He looked into her eyes and saw the unshed tears. "Not quite. Your legs aren't straight yet. Pull your toes back." He slowly eased her knee lower. "Want me to massage the cramp out?"

"No!" She groaned as Colin pulled the toe of her shoe toward her body. Her body tensed.

"You've got to relax, Nikki. Drink some of the water. You're probably dehydrated." He watched her hesitate. "What's wrong? Do you want your own bottle?"

She nodded and he crawled to her bike. "There's not much left though," she said. "I forgot to refill it in town."

Colin pulled a new bottle from the pack under the seat of his own bike and handed it to her. "Here you go. Guzzle it. And when you get home, drink a lot more milk and one of those electrolyte drinks. Eat some bananas . . ."

"Yes, sir." Nikki raised her hand in salute. She tried to stretch, but couldn't keep her leg straight while she pulled it toward her body. "Help."

Colin raised her leg off the ground and wrapped his hands around her calf, massaging it lightly as he pressed the knee straight with his elbow. As she relaxed, he stretched her leg a little more, slowly flexing her foot to pull the cramp out. Half an hour later Nikki still couldn't walk without limping. "Why don't I go get the car and come get you?"

"I need to work it out, the sooner the better," she moaned, hanging on to Colin's shoulder. He tried to wrap his arm around her waist to help her stay balanced, but she pushed him away and struggled to get to the bicycle by herself.

He liked Nikki and enjoyed the gentle sparring between them. He knew that when the relay was over, he would want to see her again. But he wasn't at all comfortable about her participation. Especially not now. "There's no need to push yourself so hard. We aren't trying to set a record. You sure Mr. Chapman wouldn't be just as happy with you riding with the trainers?"

She put her hand on his shoulder again as she lifted her feet to the pedals. "I never missed one day of practice for blisters or cramps until my ACL snapped. But I'm fine now. Just steady me while I get on the bike."

He held the bicycle while she climbed aboard, then ran alongside as she tested her riding. When it appeared she was going to manage, he swatted her the way he had his teammates in baseball. "Oh, sorry. Old habit." She continued down the path in silence while he ran back to get his cycle and catch up.

She made it back to the outlet mall going a slow and steady pace. They had met at the gym and loaded the bikes onto his rack for the drive up to the mountains. This would be a good opportunity to take her home and find out a little more about her.

"It doesn't look like the shelter is going to work out tonight."

"I know I should be nursing my leg back to health, but I agreed to watch the kids and give the parents time to go to the workshop together." She rubbed her calf and took another drink of water. "Would it be too much to ask you to drop me off at the shelter? Maybe you would like to help for a while?"

If only she knew what she was asking. "I was just thinking about that. No promises how long I'll last, but I'll give it a try."

Nikki felt her heart race and her palms turn clammy. "I didn't expect to handle the different environment well, either. Maybe it was that instant connection with Jasmine and her mother that hooked me, I don't know. It feels good to help someone." What was it that made Colin so uncomfortable with the shelter? "I hate when people are so presumptuous that they try to analyze someone they hardly know, so I'll have to trust that if it bothers you too much, you'll just leave me there. Agreed?"

"I'll agree if you promise not to jump to any conclusions." The car turned quiet and Nikki felt the awkwardness suffocating them as blocks stretched to miles before she thought of a safe topic again.

"What do you think of staying at the gym tomorrow?"

He answered without taking his eyes off the road. "I think you should give it a rest."

"I will. Tonight. By tomorrow afternoon I'll be ready for a light workout." After she got home from the shelter, she'd drink a quart of milk, then soak in a relaxing mineral bath and give her body a nice long rest. "If I take too long off, I'll have a tougher time getting back at it. I'd rather keep up an easy pace for a couple of days and then progress to a full regimen again."

"It's your call, you know the risks as well as I do. If you change your mind, I'll understand," he said compassionately.

"Don't let me slow you down, Colin. If you want to come back up here and ride . . ."

Colin turned off the interstate and headed downtown. "Whether we like it or not, Nikki, we're in this together. We have two choices, we can make peace with that, and each other, or we can let our differences work against us. Despite how I feel about visiting the shelter, I'm behind this project one hundred percent, and to me, that means we're a team . . ." They came to a stoplight and Colin turned to her.

His declaration sent warning signals through her, until she reminded herself that he didn't mean it literally or permanently. "I agree," she said, hoping her voice was steadier than her emotions. "That's why I don't want to take any more time to rest and baby this leg. I can't let you or the shelter down."

His gaze held hers with a glint of wonder. "What about Mr. Chapman?"

A horn beeped, breaking the moment. He eased the car forward, slowly, as if he wasn't sure where he was going.

"Of course, I don't want to let him down, either, but he has much less to lose at this point. If we're going to the shelter, don't we need to get into the left lane?"

"I'm sure the parents will understand that you can't watch the kids tonight. I think you should drink some electrolytes for your leg right away."

"I'll get a glass of milk at the shelter and pick up some sports drink on my way home.

Heat gets the blood circulating again and I have a heat pack in the car, which is outside the shelter. It's only for an hour. Besides, if you came to the shelter with me, we could divide and conquer the kids by ages. I could sit and read with the preschoolers, and you could help the older ones with homework — or the other way around if you'd like. You said you don't mind the kids, and that's all I agreed to help with."

Fine lines deepened on his forehead and he shook his head. Something about the shelter really bothered him.

"Forget I asked. Just drop me off and I'll manage."

Pulling to a stop in front of the old building, Colin hesitated before turning the ignition off. He got out of the car and walked around it, then took her hand, steadying her as she shifted the weight to her bum leg. She took a deep breath and held it.

"Hurts that bad?"

It just figured that he would notice. "It'll be fine, just as soon as I get moving again."

He looked at the entrance to the shelter, then back at her. "Stairs ought to be real helpful for the healing process."

"You don't need to wait, I'll make it inside." She let out her breath, hoping she could prove him wrong. She turned toward her car and took a painful step.

"Where are your keys? I'll find the heat pack for you."

She dug her keys from her bag. "There's a red box of those disposable heat packs in the glove box." She'd gotten them for her monthly cramps, but he didn't need to know that. Colin returned a few minutes later and peeled the paper off the self-stick flaps and knelt next to her. "Where do you want it, around the calf like this, or vertically along the back of your leg, like this?" Colin spun and turned the pack, testing the different options before he attached the tape to her skin.

Nikki laughed. "It looks ridiculous either way."

"Yes, it does," he said with a nod. "But looks aren't everything."

"Wrap it around, I'll live with the humiliation."

He turned the white cotton wrap and slid it along her calf. "Higher or lower?"

"Stop there. That's fine."

His rough fingers gently pressed the adhesive to her shin, sending a shiver up her leg. She avoided looking at him, afraid that he'd see the stars his gentleness put in her eyes. "Thank you for your patience," Nikki said as she stepped away from the car. "Call me in the morning and let me know what you'd like to do."

Before she realized what was happening Colin had swooped her into his arms. "Hang on," he said as he climbed the steps. "Catch the door, would you?"

"Colin! Put me down." He didn't respond immediately, and she wondered if his heart was racing as fast as hers.

"What do you say?"

"Please and thank you," she said, an unwelcome smile teasing her mouth. "But you shouldn't have done that."

"And what would you rather I did, leave you crippled and sitting on the steps in this neighborhood?" She could see his unspoken questions turn to concern as a scruffy man walked by.

"Money for a meal?" the man asked.

Colin raised his hand and shook his head and the man walked on by. "I'm sorry, Nikki, but you have a lot to learn about me."

"That didn't come out right, either." She didn't mean to insult him. "I'm overly cautious, being new to the city. And with this being business, I need to stay objective about the assignment. And . . ." And you, she almost said.

Colin stared at her with steely determination, and then he left.

She wasn't ready to face this kind of disappointment yet. Maybe, just maybe, if he could get to know her better, he'd realize she wasn't like the other women who had obviously left him jaded. And given time, she might convince herself that he wasn't only interested in her grandfather's money, either.

Nikki started toward the front room of the shelter on her own, reflecting on the many ways Colin had surprised her. He'd been caring and protective, and except for that confusing slap on the back, the perfect gentleman.

So why had he gone to such great lengths to make sure she was comfortable, only to walk away from families who needed so much more than a warm patch on the leg?

Chapter Nine

Colin sat in his car waiting and watching for Nikki. Why, he wasn't sure. He was worried about her, but knew she wasn't his responsibility. Just swallow your pride and go help her. It won't kill you.

He pressed his head back against the seat and groaned. *"Wasn't once in a lifetime enough, Lord?"* The clock on the dash said it was only seven-thirty. Go inside.

He made it only as far as the steps before the doubt returned. Raised voices streamed out the opened windows in unison. He could remember the musty smell of the cots, and how much he'd missed his own bed. His parents had fought more those three months than any time before or since. He and his brother and sister were in new schools because of the unexpected move, and thus were teased during recess, when teachers' backs were turned. It bothered him that after twenty years, the memories were so vivid. He felt the embarrassment as his father forced Colin to turn down a friend's parents' offer to pay for Colin to join the youth baseball program that summer.

The kids inside could use an understanding friend, just like you did.

He wasn't eleven anymore, and he wasn't about to make the same mistakes most people made when dealing with the needy. He knew firsthand what it was like to feel unwanted and invisible.

Before he could back out again, Colin sneaked inside. Nikki, surrounded by little girls and boys, appeared to have engaged an entire staff of nurses and doctors. She had a toy thermometer held up to her face, a beanbag on her head, and a blanket over her legs.

Colin leaned his shoulder against the door frame and watched quietly. The dining room had been converted to a classroom where parents were practicing, according to the calendar, "good communication and bad communication methods." He'd obviously heard the bad communications from outside.

Jasmine, the little girl they had met a few days earlier, had climbed into Nikki's lap and was running her fingers through Nikki's hair.

An even smaller toddler crawled over to her leg and patted the heat pack on her leg. "Ooh, hot," the boy exclaimed. The gleam in his brown eyes could be seen from across the room.

A teenage girl engaged several children by reading a story about a mother bear adopting a baby alligator, a beaver and a funny-looking bird to make a happy family.

Huddled in a corner across the room, a young boy bounced a basketball against the wall, ignoring the rest of the chaos. Colin found his mission. He crossed the room, nodding to Nikki as he passed by. She grabbed the beanbag from her head and jumped to attention.

"C—"

He pressed his index finger over his lips, telling her to be quiet. "I have someone to visit. Carry on." She relaxed back onto the sofa and smiled.

Not wanting to be distracted, Colin positioned himself next to the young man, keeping his back to Nikki and the rest of the kids.

"Hi, I'm Colin. Is there someplace we can shoot some hoops?"

The kid shook his head. "Nope. Can't go outside after dark," he said without looking up. "This place stinks. It's like some cage or prison or somethin'."

"Mind if I sit with you for a few minutes?"

"Don't matter to me what you do."

Colin pulled up an old oak chair and straddled it, leaning his chin on the back.

"How long have you been here?"

He shrugged. "Too long to keep track of."

"Eighty-five days, seven hours and twelve minutes was my record. I was about your age, too. That was a long time ago. What's your name?"

"Yeah, right." He studied Colin from head to toe. "Name's Mike. That's about as funny as imagining *her* homeless." He pointed to Nikki. "You weren't really, were you?"

"It can happen to any of us, me, her, your teacher . . ." Colin hoped that sharing his own challenges would make a difference for Mike and his attitude. "You know, Mike, sometimes it isn't so much what we do right or wrong that gets us here, it's often things that happen out of our control. If I had given up then, I wouldn't be living comfortably now."

Before too long, Colin and the boy had opened a textbook and Colin was helping him with his algebra.

Nikki yawned as she heard the parent group meeting close in prayer. The baby had fallen asleep in her lap, and she was afraid to move for fear of waking him.

"Jory, Jazzy, can you help put the toys back in the tub?" The kids immediately got busy and had the room relatively clean by the time the doors to the dining room opened and their parents led them away to the dorms. Nikki was shocked to see how quickly and quietly the place emptied. Kathleen thanked Nikki for helping, and Colin for seeking out the young man.

"It's especially difficult to cope with homelessness at his age."

Colin glanced at Nikki and then at Kathleen and nodded. "I know how it is for him," he said, watching their puzzled looks deepen. He realized then that Mike would probably tell if he didn't. "My family spent almost three months in a shelter when I was eleven. I don't especially want to let that out, but I realize it might help Mike to see that people can overcome these situations."

"That's why it was so difficult for you to come in here, isn't it?" Nikki suspected Colin's background would be in the news before the week's end, but she was determined it wouldn't be from her telling it.

"I wish we had more helpers like you two," Kathleen said. "Any time you need a break, you're welcome here." She said goodbye and excused herself.

After they left the shelter Colin became very quiet. "I'm not going to include that in the articles, if you're wondering," Nikki finally stated.

"Thanks," he said quietly. "Pride isn't an easy flaw to overcome. As much as it hurt and embarrassed me when my dad's pride got in the way, you'd think I wouldn't have that same problem."

"I promised I wouldn't analyze you, so I won't pretend to have an answer for you. I can only observe that I'm very impressed that you opened up in order to help someone else."

He shook his head. "Don't be. It took me twenty years to get the courage to do it. Let me follow you home, just to make sure the car runs okay."

She shook her head. "You don't have to do that. It's a good neighborhood."

"The car?"

"I'm going car shopping as soon as I get time."

"I bet you have stairs to climb, don't you? And I'd hate for you to have to try to get your bike out of the trunk by yourself. It wouldn't take me more than a minute to deliver it for you."

Nikki smiled. "Fine, follow me home. Then I can prove to you that I can manage okay on my own."

A few minutes later they drove to her

condo on the cusp of the affluent Cherry Hills area. She heard the garage door close and jumped. Colin appeared next to her. "I put your bicycle just inside the door of the garage. Hope that's okay."

"Thanks," she said, wondering if he'd also seen her not-so-modest convertible at the opposite side of the garage.

He leaned his shoulder against the corner of the garage, placed one hand on his hip and lowered his eyes. "I'm sorry for the . . ." he paused to lick his lips ". . . well, for the pat." He held out his hand, as if it had acted on its own, then crossed his arms over his chest, tucking his hands under his arms. "And the dinner invitation. I didn't realize you were seeing anyone."

Nikki hobbled over to him. "What makes you think I am?"

"The second car in the garage."

"So you think I'm living with someone because I have two cars in my garage?"

"What?" He shrugged. "I didn't say that."

"I clearly saw you examining my left hand during lunch. And since there's no ring, you know I'm not married."

He shook his head. "That's not what I meant, either." He shrugged, releasing his hands and holding them in front of him.

"For all I know, it's a roommate's, a platonic . . ."

"Why don't you just ask next time you want to know something. It's my old car." She realized that he wouldn't be able to tell what exact model it was, as she had it covered to protect the paint. "I'm not dating anyone right now, nor do I intend to."

"I'm sorry, Nikki," he said awkwardly. "I didn't mean to offend you."

She backed away, tripping herself and she landed on the ground. "Ouch."

Colin immediately reached out a hand and hoisted her to her feet again, stepping farther away as she regained her footing.

"That didn't come out right, either." She didn't mean to insult him. "I'm overly cautious, being new to the city. And with this . . . us . . . being business, I need to stay objective about the assignment."

Before she could correct herself they were both stopped in their tracks by a giant bouquet on her steps. This one, however, wasn't the small apology-type bouquet. This one was outrageously large and disturbingly familiar. The tropical flowers could only be from one person. Rory.

It had been two years since she'd seen him. What was he doing here? And what did he want from her now?

"This looks like a good time to say good night," Colin said as he spun around and drove off.

Chapter Ten

Negotiations on using the highway had dragged on through the summer, with delays caused by road construction and maintenance problems. Finally, the approval needed to complete the fund-raiser came through. Unfortunately, the fund-raiser now found itself in a race against Mother Nature as well. Finally, all of the pieces came together and the team was ready to go.

Colin loaded a case of sports drinks into the cooler, then poured a bag of ice cubes over the top. Nikki would be here soon, and he couldn't believe how nervous he was to see her after five days.

He recalled the bouquet sitting on her front step. She sure had a funny perspective on dating, if the guy who sent it wasn't a boyfriend. A bouquet like that made his little arrangement look like the peanuts he'd pushed through downtown Denver. He felt like a fool, but it probably saved a lot of pain and effort in the long run.

Oddly enough, they hadn't been able to work out a time since that day to train together, though he had seen her name on the gym sign-in charts several days. Though she had him beat when it came to stamina, she was hurting when it came to cross-training.

Surely the old man had more faith in him than to really expect anyone to suffer through every mile of agony right by his side, but what Nikki lacked in skill, she made up for in determination. The word *quit* was not in Nikki Post's vocabulary, despite blisters, muscle cramps or bone-jolting falls.

"The bikes are ready," Jared said, startling Colin. He glared at his friend, who looked confused. "What's wrong with you today? That's not the first time I've said something to make you jump."

"Pregame jitters, I guess." Colin did not want to admit to Jared that he'd been thinking about — let alone worrying about — a woman, when he had been turning down blind dates for the past year. "I wish Mr. Chapman hadn't insisted a reporter participate. It's enough to worry about myself through these events."

From Jared's expression, he didn't believe Colin's excuse. "I hope it's not some old geezer that we're going to be nursing along this whole trip."

"Not hardly. You really don't know who

the reporter is?" Colin said in honest disbelief. Somehow he and Nikki had missed Jared and Sandra at the gym. "How did you bring the right size equipment for her?"

"Her?" Jared said with a chuckle. "So that's what has you jumpy today. The secretary at the newspaper called last week to find out what equipment would be needed. I told her we had what you needed and she said they would make sure to get the reporter the proper equipment for the job. What's that supposed to mean, anyway?" Jared tossed Colin's pogo stick and the tricycles into the trailer.

"What does it sound like it means?"

Jared thought a minute. "It sounds like you have a shadow." One look at Colin and he couldn't stifle his laughter.

A shadow of temptation, little as Colin liked to admit it. Since introducing him to Nikki was Jared and Sandra's idea in the first place, Colin could guarantee it was going to be a long week. The newspaper van pulled up and Colin turned his attention back to Jared. Sandra stepped out of the motor home, smiling. "Hey, the gang's all here."

A white-haired woman got out of the passenger's side and lifted her camera. "Smile, Colin!" Ellis got out of the driver's seat and walked around the van, with Gary, the journalist Nikki would report to on this story.

Jared's expression said it all. "I guess the joke is on you, it is an old geezer," he whispered, turning his back to the van, rolling his eyes. "So much for it being some cutie."

Colin gave a quick nod. "Look again."

Jared's eyes popped open. He threw his hands in the air in surrender, right before he looked at Colin with that "Don't blame me for this one" look, followed by laughter. Even Jared couldn't have faked his surprise that well. "The Lord works in some pretty amazing ways," Jared whispered with a wicked laugh.

"Afternoon, Nikki," Colin said, offering her a hand with her bags. He couldn't believe how much he'd missed seeing her.

She grabbed a duffel bag and an overstuffed briefcase from the seat beside her. "Hi," she said quietly. "I just have these. Where should I put them?"

Colin hated to admit how good it was to see her again and did all he could to hide his feelings for her. She'd made herself very clear that until the relay was over, they needed to concentrate on business. Why, he still had to figure out.

"Come on in," Sandra said, smiling from

ear to ear. "I'll help you unpack in *our* room."

"You knew, too?" Jared shook his head, then turned to Colin when the women went into the motor home. "I thought Sandra was joking when she said you and I would have the pullout beds. I can't believe neither of you told me Nikki would be coming along." Jared turned to Colin. "So why are you worried about Nikki? She'll do fine."

"Did you know she'd had surgery on her ACL?"

Jared nodded. "And it's doing fine."

Colin made introductions as Ellis unloaded athletic equipment from the back of the minivan and handed it to Jared and Colin. "I hope these are adequate to get Nicole through the relay."

"Looks like you spared nothing to get the best," Jared quipped. "I didn't know Nikki was a reporter."

Ellis looked into the empty van, closed the hatch, then turned back to them. "It's her first assignment. If I didn't trust Colin to extend her the courtesy of his years of journalism experience I wouldn't have chosen her. Nikki will be keeping in contact with Gary Richardson during the relay."

Gary lifted a camera and snapped photos, along with the white-haired woman. Colin introduced himself to both, surprised to discover the latter was none other than Mrs. Chapman. He'd not thought to make introductions, but it seemed everyone was taking care of that themselves.

Jared said, "I'm the owner of Jared's Gym. And my wife is one of Nikki's trainers."

Colin watched and listened curiously as the two men sang Nikki accolades of admiration. As if on cue Sandra and Nikki joined them and a small group from the shelter gathered to launch the Back on Track Relay. Kathleen led a small group, including Mike and a few other young adults. The media pulled him, Kathleen and Ellis together and interviewed them regarding the joint venture.

The camera came out and publicity photos again threw Colin into the limelight. Jared examined and loaded Nikki's equipment. The sound man from WWJD radio handed Colin a minirecorder to record journal entries along the route.

"Let's get this show on the road," Ellis's voice boomed over the crowd. Ellis handed a digital camera to Nikki. "I still wish we had a cameraman going along," he added. "It would be good to have both of you in some of the pictures."

"It's a tight fit as it is," Colin reminded the publisher. "We promised the highway department we'd interrupt the traffic flow as little as possible, and with a motor home, trailer and pedestrian traffic, I'd say we have enough to create a minor disruption. The director has made enough allowances for us as it is." Colin shook Ellis's hand, noting Nikki's raised eyebrow as she glanced to Ellis and his wife.

Sandra interrupted with her assurance that she'd get pictures for Ellis to use for publicity and Nikki quietly protested using her picture. Mr. Chapman nodded with a peculiar twitch of his lip. "You take good care of Nicole, Colin." He cleared his throat. "And all of you be careful out there."

Nikki's smile was tight-lipped as she awkwardly leaned forward and gave Ellis, then his wife, quick, impersonal hugs. "I'll give it my all," she said softly.

"I know you will, Nicole," Ellis said, patting her shoulder. "You always do." He followed them to the door of the motor home, folding the aluminum steps beneath the vehicle. "We'll look forward to hearing from you."

Finally they closed the door of the motor home and stood in the plush living room facing one another. "So, who's driving?" Jared asked, looking at Colin. "You arranged for the rig, you drive."

"I thought you were taking the driving course they arranged," Colin said innocently.

"There were lessons?"

Nikki's eyes opened wider.

Sandra shook her head and gave her husband a push. "Get up there and quit joking around. Nikki, there's one thing you may as well know right now. These two have been pulling this routine since they were teenagers. They love a fresh audience."

"And you'd think Sandra would know better than to blow it after five years," Jared said with a smile. "Why don't you two start out in the captain's seat, enjoy an easy ride while you can."

Colin's broad smile accentuated his bronzed skin. "Sounds like a deal. Ladies first." He motioned for Nikki to have a seat. "Only the best for our copilot." He sat down in the driver's chair and turned it toward hers. "Let me give you a tour of our pilot's cabin. Swivel seats for ease of loading and unloading. They need to be locked in the forward position prior to takeoff." He gestured to the lever on the side of her chair with a sweeping motion of his sculpted arm.

"This lever locks it, this one adjusts the seat, this button is the lumbar control, and this —" he paused, his eyes meeting hers "— is the ejector button."

She both loved and hated his deep blue eyes. She wondered how anyone could not be drawn into the warmth and compassion swimming within them. Still, she hated their magnetic pull because it was impossible not to look into them and smile, especially with the goofy grin he was sporting now. "Do I control that, or do you?"

"Oh, no, that's yours to control. Lest you forget, though, it's your job to make sure the pilot conforms to all regulations, you know. There is no automatic pilot, so you can't get rid of me." His smile widened to the point she didn't think possible. "For your comfort today we have individual air setting controls so I don't freeze you out. Heated leather seats for the end of the day when our muscles need a little help. Hmm." He paused to play with the buttons. "Surely there's a massager in here, too." He found the right button that made the whole cabin rumble and they both started laughing. "Whoa. Not ready for that yet." They glanced outside to the onlookers watching and waiting. Her grandfather came to the window, and she searched for the button to roll it down.

"What was that awful noise?"

Nikki laughed. "Just finding out what all these buttons do. That was the massager."

Colin turned his seat toward the steering wheel and locked it into position, starting the engine. "Did I mention there's a water dispenser for keeping the pilot hydrated?"

"Now you did." Nikki's mind drifted back to the barbecue while he rambled on about the stereo and the state-of-the-art sun visors. She nodded, her mind really on the mishap that had left her with one more pair of grubby jeans and a dozen graceful calla lilies and a very generous shopping card. There was no need trying to blame the ostentatious bouquet Rory had sent on a mistaken delivery. If there was one thing she knew about men, it was that they liked competition, and the look of embarrassment on Colin's face had read "loser" all the way around. But it was probably too late to convince him that she didn't care to keep in contact with Rory Drake. She buckled her seat belt and locked her seat. "It does sort of remind you of a cockpit up here, doesn't it?"

"It's as close as I'll ever get to one. Could you inform the passengers that we're ready for takeoff." Though he was still joking around, Colin's demeanor changed with the shift of gears. The smile faded as the vehicle slowly moved forward. He tested the brakes a couple of times, then proceeded out of the empty lot next to the current shelter.

"Buckle up back there, Colin's turning." She smiled. "Not that I don't trust you."

Colin let out a low whistle. "I see how it's going to be. Just remember, I can dish it out, too."

Nikki laughed. "Which reminds me, I think I owe you an apology. I realized I never thanked you for the beautiful flowers and gift certificate you sent. You didn't have to send either, but I did enjoy both."

"Oh, I see how it is. Lower my defenses, then be nice." His smile returned. "You know what happens when I'm thrown off balance." His brows furrowed as he maneuvered through the traffic.

"Yeah, I get to go shopping." She cringed. That sounded like a selfish rich-girl thing to say. I don't need any more strikes against me than I already have, she thought. She turned to look back at Jared and Sandra, sitting on the sofa watching the television. "Speaking of the barbecue, who's taking care of Lizzy this week?"

"My parents are watching her. I didn't think you two needed any extra handicap."

Colin turned onto the interstate and merged carefully into the bumper-to-bumper traffic. “Better turn on the radio station, I think we’re going to need some prayers.”

Chapter Eleven

The past two mornings Nikki had watched Colin disappear over the side of the mountain and return an hour later in a good mood. It didn't take a rocket scientist to figure out that he had been starting his day meditating or praying or whatever devout believers did that made them impossibly joyful first thing in the morning.

Today Nikki decided to find her own solitude, but searched for a spot farther away from camp where she could concentrate on what Grandfather had told her. She perched on the smooth rock beneath the rustling leaves of the aspen trees to watch another glorious Colorado sunrise. The golden prairie turned magnificent shades of lavender, pink and fuchsia, thanks to a few clouds that had passed over during the night. She tugged the zipper of her fleece jacket higher. Even in Denver, September was a time of warm days and cool nights, but here in the mountains it felt like a more drastic change of season was on the way.

She pulled her feet onto the rock in front of her and hugged her legs close to her body.

One minute Colin and Jared were debating serious national issues, the next they were pulling pranks on each other as if they were teenagers at summer camp.

Though both sides of Colin's personality impressed her as intelligent and entertaining, his relationship with God left her totally intimidated. It didn't bother her when Colin had blessed the food before each meal or when she'd heard him humming songs now and then that she'd never heard before. But when she made the mistake of asking about the tune, all three of them had broken into song about an awesome God, then placed a compact disc in the stereo and blasted Christian music as if they were at a rock concert. She didn't mind the music so much, but this unfamiliar side of her travel partners left her feeling very uncomfortable.

"I am way out of my element here," Nikki whispered. "How am I going to get out of this?" God was for Sunday mornings and making donations. She folded her hands over her knees and studied the changing sunrise. The sun's rays shot up from the billowy cloud like fingers reaching toward Heaven, outlining the scalloped top edge of the gray clouds with such a brilliant white light that she finally understood where the image of the silver lining came from. How could she discount God's power while looking at such beauty? And even if she did acknowledge her own beliefs, she had no connection to a particular church. Though she knew she'd be welcomed with open arms, she still didn't feel comfortable going to her grandparents' church. Where did one start?

"Morning, mind if I join you?" Colin had that annoying smile plastered on his face already.

She shook her head, then looked around, realizing she had occupied the only safe and comfortable perch on the rocky slope. "I can move . . ."

"Don't . . ."

". . . so you can have your privacy." She didn't know what he really did out here each morning, and didn't want to intrude.

"I don't want privacy, or I wouldn't have hiked all over the mountain looking for you."

"Oh." She scooted over and Colin didn't wait for an invitation to sit next to her. "Is there a problem?" she asked.

"That was my question for you. Is it my imagination, or have you been really uncomfortable the past day or so? You hardly said a word at dinner last night."

"That's not so strange." She concentrated on the horizon, disappointed to see how quickly her image of reaching out to God faded away. For a moment, it seemed as if she could see forever. If only it were that easy to see into her future, to know what she was supposed to do from here. She glanced at Colin.

He laughed, but the look in his eyes was that of concern. "No, you're pretty quiet most of the time, which makes it all that more apparent when you're upset."

How had he even noticed, as bubbly and gregarious as he, Jared and Sandra were? There was hardly a chance to get a word in edgewise.

"I don't want to start today until we clear the air. If I've upset you I want to apologize."

"No," she mumbled as she shook her head. "It's not something you've done." It's who you are, she thought. And who I'm not. From her experience if something was too good to be true, it usually was. Which was why Colin confused her so. He was smart and witty, handsome and generous. What wasn't to like about him? In her circle, men who were so smooth usually had a very slick side to them, as well. And she always seemed to attract the slickest of them.

"What is it then? Something has upset you."

She admired him and his concern. "I just . . ." She hesitated, not wanting to admit that his faith in God left her feeling an inch tall. "I feel very out of place. You all talk about God in such a different way than I've ever experienced." She stopped suddenly. She hadn't meant to tell him that, hadn't even figured it out completely. Where had that come from? Colin wasn't responding, and she didn't have the courage to look at him or ask if she'd really said that last part aloud. Maybe she was just imagining it.

"I kind of suspected that was it."

Nikki longed to understand why her grandfather had been praying for her. She wasn't a bad person. She hadn't married the wrong man. She didn't misuse and flaunt her money, as Colin had implied his ex-girlfriend had. Still, she couldn't ask just anyone her many questions. Though her grandparents meant well, they too had a way of piling expectations on her shoulders, and the vicious cycle of pleasing everyone else started again.

Colin wrapped his arm around her and pulled her close. "I understand how you feel, Nikki. I remember the first time I met what was then called a 'born-again' Christian. It was during my rehabilitation from my baseball injury. Bill wasn't going to walk again, and yet he was so disgustingly happy I thought he was either a kook or on some pretty strong medications. Sound familiar?"

She shrugged, trying to hide her smile. "Sort of."

"He was confined to the rehab center at that time and I was living at home, going in for my appointments. I tried everything I could to get on a different schedule to avoid him, but every time, something came up to put us in physical therapy together. He'd heard of my injury, and knew as much about my baseball stats as I did. He even knew about my stay in the shelter as a kid. So I was really spooked for the first few days. I was convinced Bill was out to end my career, and I was sure my dad's ugly temper would come back to haunt us all."

"You were that good?" She couldn't help the surprise in her voice. "I mean . . ."

His laughter came from deep down in his chest. "You're not the first one to be surprised that I had a successful past, but it was one of those careers that sounds more glamorous than it really was."

"I'm sorry. That was rude of me." Her grandfather's lecture came back to her —

"judge not that ye be not judged." The very thing that bothered her, and she was most guilty of doing the same to others. In fact, she was worse. She wouldn't even let him know who she was so he could judge her. "I'm so sorry, Colin . . ."

He placed a finger beneath her chin and turned her face to his. His eyes alone betrayed his ardor, yet he quickly suppressed that and changed the subject. "I was telling you about Bill, wasn't I?"

She nodded, reminded that she'd not only insulted him, but she'd also disregarded his story, caught up in discovering this joy-filled man had his own secrets.

"I came to trust Bill. I'm not sure who was more tickled, him to meet me, or me to meet my first true fan. His hometown was near mine, so he had followed all of the hype since high school. There were a lot of expectations for me and my career all along. Except from my parents. Whenever I started thinking too much of myself, they wasted no time planting my feet back on earth."

"They didn't want you to play baseball?"

"They enjoy baseball for what it is, a game. And like so many Americans, they think there's way too much hype and money invested in sports. They were happy for me, but I think my talent caught them off guard, too. Once I made it to the pros, they had to face reality — my pipe dream was real. And once they saw the pressure involved they regretted encouraging my competitiveness at all."

Nikki felt a jealous pang. "I'm sure that wasn't easy, but at least you got to see for yourself what it was like to reach your dream."

He nodded. "I'm grateful for that, but nothing comes without a price. It was a wild time, and I don't regret the experience, but I'm much happier out of the high-pressured limelight."

"You had a choice about going back?"

Colin shrugged. "In a manner of speaking. I wouldn't have been able to stay at my former pro level for long. I was pretty bitter company for quite a while. I thought my future was ending before it started. My rehab buddy made me realize God wasn't closing a door, He'd opened a world of opportunities through baseball. Even the injury opened doors I wouldn't have considered before God took the driver's seat of my life, including this one. No one would care if we were here raising money for anyone, except that it started with the bonus of an ex-ballplayer overcoming his injury. God gave me the talent and allows me to use His gifts to benefit His plan.

"Sometimes I get a little carried away with my enthusiasm, like yesterday. Here I'm doing something I consider just as fun as baseball and it's going to glorify God when all is said and done. That's only part of why I love my new job so much. I enjoy sharing the joy of God's love and grace. If it's not too personal to ask — do you believe in God?"

She looked into the sky and back at the prairie. "How can anyone *not* believe in God?" She shrugged. "Of course I do."

"I don't mean to intimidate you. Everyone comes from different perspectives in their faith, and I don't mind that."

"You don't mind what?" She looked into his eyes as if they were the stormy ocean. "Why should you care what I believe in the first place?"

"I guess I should say I understand we all come from different backgrounds, in life and in our religious beliefs. And I'm curious about where you might be in your walk with God because I care about you."

"We may have spent a lot of time together, but you *hardly* know me. And for that matter, I only know what everyone in the country knows about Colin Wright, only what you want us to know, which is very little."

Colin rested his hands on his knees and tapped his fingers. "It doesn't mean we can't get to know each other better, does it?"

Nikki couldn't respond. If he knew everything about her he wouldn't want to spend another day together. She wanted him to know Ellis Chapman was her grandfather, yet if she told him, how would she ever know if he cared for her for who she was and not because of her family connections? Colin had a bright career ahead of him, and it was becoming very clear that Grandfather liked him, too. She felt as though she was caught between bases, and was about to be tagged out. But if she told Colin who she really was now, she wouldn't feel so guilty. "There's . . ."

"Why don't we take it one day at a time? No pressure, no rush, and if you want to know anything about me, just ask. As long as we can agree that my personal life doesn't go into the article, I'll answer anything. Could we pray together?" Colin reached out his hand for hers.

His fingers were strong and warm, making her feel secure and safe, but even more guilty.

"You're cold. Let's get out of this breeze first."

"No, I'm fine. Go ahead and pray now," she said, turning to him. It was awkward enough with the two of them, she didn't want two more sets of eyes witness to her ignorance. "And Colin, would you not talk to Sandra and Jared about what we talked about? I feel so stupid. My parents only took us to church on holidays, and trust me, back then there was no music like you guys have now."

"You can't be expected to know what you haven't been exposed to. If there's anything you don't understand, ask. God loves you, Nikki, and I can't deny that I'm feeling something pretty special for you, too."

Chapter Twelve

Colin took her hand in his and bowed his head. *"Almighty Father, we praise this day you have given us and the beautiful countryside. Allow everything we do to glorify you and your plans. Bless our journey and give Nikki and me strength to persevere so that others may have shelter over their heads. . . ."*

Nikki listened while Colin asked God to come into their presence because the two of them were gathered in His name. Silently, she added her own request that she would find the peace and joy that He had given Colin. She missed the end of Colin's prayer, hearing him say only, "Amen."

He let go of her hand and climbed back over the boulder, offering her assistance.

"I'm fine, thanks." She looked at her watch. They had just enough time to make another bathroom break and add a Windbreaker to her layers before she needed to check in with Gary. He'd hinted that there could be a break in the fight over the land. "So what did you decide we should ride today?"

"The majority of it is downhill, so I thought we could get the tricycle out of the way. What do you think?"

Colin and Jared had done most of the research and planning for the relay. She wasn't about to interfere with their work. "I'm with you all the way, just let me know what I need to do."

She followed him back to camp, where Jared and Sandra had the equipment ready and waiting.

Nikki went into the motor home, called Gary, grabbed her jacket and went to the refrigerator to get a bottle of sports drink. Everything was warm. She set it back and put the Windbreaker on, meeting the crew outside. "Did you know the refrigerator isn't working?"

Jared produced two bottles of cold drink from the ice chest. "Yeah, we noticed. I've called the dealer and they gave us some suggestions. If we can't find the problem, we'll have it checked out in Pueblo. We'll work on that while you two start down the mountain. Go on to the top of the pass and we'll meet you on the north side of Walsenburg. Cell phones . . ."

Colin looked at his. "Have service."

"Water?"

Colin looked at both tricycles, raising his

backpack from the platform between the back tires. "Check."

Sandra tugged on Jared's arm. "You've checked everything else there is to check. Get going and good luck," she said impatiently.

Nikki looked at Colin with the tricycle and laughed. "I need a picture of this." She pulled out the digital camera Grandfather had given her and waited for Colin to climb on.

"I think you're supposed to be in the photo as well, aren't you?" Sandra reached for the camera.

Nikki and Colin wheeled up side by side and smiled while Sandra snapped a picture in front of the Back on Track banner. She examined it on the screen and gave them the thumbs-up. "You're off . . ."

"Like a herd of turtles." Nikki put her feet on the pedals and struggled to get her knees out of the way while Colin moved along toward the exit to the campground with his feet on the ground. "Hey, you have to ride, not walk. Cheater!"

"We aren't using motors, and I'm not walking, I'm coasting." He laughed. "Besides, we aren't to the top of the pass yet, so technically we could walk the trike to the highway before we even have to get on."

"Oh, yeah. Good idea," she agreed. "No need going through any more agony than we have to."

A few minutes later they had both made it to the crest of Raton Pass and scrunched their legs to get their feet onto the pedals. "Is this really the largest tricycle they make?"

"I guarantee it. The salesman thought Jared and I were a little off our rockers when we climbed on every one."

"I can imagine. I'm still questioning that myself, but I do admire your courage." She pushed off and straightened her legs in front of her, letting the pedals go free.

"Did I hear you say you admire me?" Colin mimicked her, tipping over when he tried to pull his legs onto the handlebars. "Whoa. Hold up!"

Nikki glanced over her shoulder and dropped her feet to the gravel-sprinkled asphalt, skidding to a halt. Colin picked himself up off the ground with that daring teenage smile on his face. Nikki stopped. "Are you okay?"

He brushed sand from his leg and arm, then climbed back onto the trike and straightened his baseball cap. "Ready."

Nikki looked to the east and the long bumpy ride they'd have if they fell over the side. "I think we'd better keep our feet on the pedals and take this a bit more seriously."

"You're not into mountain biking, huh?"

She smiled and gave him the familiar refrain. "No, I danced." She pulled her knees to her body and put her feet on the pedals again. "How many miles do we have to ride these things?"

"Don't think about it. It's mostly downhill, so I hoped we could take advantage of that and get a little credit for the next time we get the trike on the schedule."

She considered her role here as bean counter and wondered if anyone would know the difference if they traded the trikes' time for one of the other transportation gimmicks. "I love the idea, but I'm afraid that we'll lose track of how many miles we've ridden each. There is a set rotation, isn't there?"

"Yeah, but the next rotation is Rollerblades. Then come pogo sticks and scooters. I don't remember the exact order."

" 'Nuf said. The tricycle works for me. There's no way I'm going down a mountain pass on my first attempt at cross-country blading. Not without a rail on the side of the road, anyway."

Sandra and Jared followed in the motor home with a flashing light and a banner warning of pedestrians on the highway shoulder.

Fifteen minutes into the ride, a gust of wind pelted them with sand, stopping them both. "Aw, man, there went my hat." Colin watched his baseball cap fly up into the blue sky and glide down the mountain into the top of a ponderosa pine twenty feet from the highway.

"You did put sunscreen on your scalp, didn't you?"

"I didn't think I needed it, I was wearing a hat."

Nikki walked her trike next to him and pulled a small sample of sunscreen from her waist pack. "You're welcome to try this. I'm not sure how good it is, it came in the mail last week."

Colin rubbed the thick white paste over his head and face. "Remind me to buy four hats in the next town," he grumbled. "If a pair is good, two will be better."

"Don't forget your ears."

He swiped over them quickly and tucked the empty packet into his leather waist pouch.

They wheeled past a ghost town where coal must have been present, as the red Colorado soil had turned to black sand. Nikki sighed as they passed the mileage sign indicating they had two hundred and ten miles to go until they reached Denver. And that was a straight shot up the interstate. They would be taking detours on the areas where the DOT required alternative routes to their destination. "I must say, I've never realized how much prairie Colorado has until now," Nikki said, watching the high bluffs turn to sagebrush and piñon pines. Traffic was light to the bottom of the pass, and Nikki couldn't wait to get off the trike. Her legs were cramping and stiff. Near as she could tell, they had only gone about five miles, and they had twenty to go. Already she wanted a hot bath. Between the wind and the vehicles passing them, they'd been pelted with sand, blown to a standstill, lost a cap, and now they felt as if they'd halfway crossed the state. Unfortunately they'd barely started.

Jared beeped the horn and Colin stumbled to the passenger's window to talk to him. "You okay?"

"Just a little stiff. There's a reason adults don't ride tricycles."

"Yeah. The engine keeps overheating in the low gear when I follow you close, so we're going to have to do something different."

"Go on ahead a mile or so and wait for us, then we'll leapfrog. Wait awhile there, let us get ahead again, and pass us. That should help. The sign does indicate we're ahead of the motor home, so that will make the drivers aware to keep watch. We'll have to make it work."

"It's been ten miles, are you ready to change to blades yet?"

"After lunch. Why don't you and Sandra get the necessary gear together and meet us when it's ready. Then we'll change."

Colin yelled ahead to Nikki to tell her the plan and they proceeded side by side. "We have another fifteen miles to go today and fairly level ground to cover. I don't know about you, but I'm ready for lunch. Sandra is going to heat something up and meet us in a mile or two."

Nikki had finished her water long ago and now guzzled the rest of her sports drink. With her legs already sore, she wasn't going to take any chances. She was parched by the dry weather. "Colin, do you have any water left?"

"Not much, but we can refill at lunch. That'll be within the hour."

Forty minutes later they hadn't seen any sign of the motor home. Colin called Jared on the cell phone, but there was no answer.

They waited just outside a town under the shade of an abandoned, boarded-up gas station. Nikki stumbled off the tricycle and grabbed hold of the rusty beam that supported a pastel-colored fiberglass awning. She arched her back and looked up at the blue sky. "Look, is that an eagle?"

Colin stepped close, wrapping his arm around her shoulder for support. "It's a bald eagle. See the white spot on his head?"

Nikki looked again. "Just so it isn't a vulture circling the doomed." She wanted to collapse from fatigue and hunger. "Where are Sandra and Jared?"

He stared at the eagle, not responding for the longest time to Nikki's question. "I hope the motor home didn't have more problems. Why don't we rest a few minutes, maybe it will help us regain some strength."

"I don't think anything can do that right now, but I'm willing to try."

Colin sat on the crumbling concrete. "Here, lean against my back and I'll keep watch for them."

Nikki hadn't the energy to argue. She leaned her head back against Colin's shoulder and closed her eyes. A while later she awoke.

"Aren't they here yet?"

"Haven't heard from them. I think we'd

better go on into town. I'm going to find a pay phone, see if it's our cell phone that's bad. Maybe we can rustle up something to eat while we're there."

"And what are you going to use for money, your good looks?"

He laughed. "Think it would work?"

"I hope so, because I didn't bring my money or credit cards with me. They're in the motor home."

Chapter Thirteen

Colin hadn't thought to carry any money or identification, either. They both groaned as they stood. "I didn't happen to miss a hot tub in the motor home, did I?"

She laughed. "It's nice, but not that nice. But it does have those heated seats with the massager. Even those sound pretty tempting right now."

Colin looked at his watch. "It's been over an hour, and they're not answering the phone. Something has to have gone wrong. Who do we call — Ellis, the State Patrol or the shelter?" Nikki shrugged. Neither had a definite answer. "And I thought we'd considered everything."

While they bounced ideas back and forth, Nikki stretched. "I vote for the State Patrol. They're the ones most likely to have responded if there was an emergency." She folded herself in half, setting her palms on the ground in front of her, stretching her quadriceps and glutes. She glanced up and caught him staring.

"Doesn't that hurt?"

She laughed. "No pain, no gain. You'd

better stretch before your muscles tighten up too much more. We should have done so before our nap." She smiled. "Yes, I know you dozed off, too. Your snore is even cuter than Sandra's, and I'd never have thought that was possible."

"Oh, yeah? I've never heard anyone call any snoring cute before." He bent over, trying to follow her lead. He wasn't nearly as limber as she was, or else he was already too stiff to stretch. His fingertips were inches from the ground. "Oh, this is agony."

She smiled. "Athletes. Why don't coaches teach you that stretching is the most important part of any training routine? Don't force it. Just go as far as is comfortable. We don't need any torn muscles."

"Nothing is comfortable today. You don't think we slept through them going by, do you? Maybe we should head on down the road."

"We're not so far off the highway that someone wouldn't notice our trikes, especially if they were looking for us. Try the phone again."

He dialed, with no better result. He pressed 411, then Send, hoping they wouldn't get an operator from New Mexico instead of locally. He confirmed his location and asked to be transferred to the non-emergency number of the State Patrol. Colin did a lunge, resting one hand against the post for support, stretching his legs with a runner's stretch. "They're connecting me."

"I don't know about you, but I suggest we donate the tricycles to a local child-care center and run instead. Another mile on that thing and I'm going to have a permanent curve in my spine."

The State Patrol line picked up, and when the man on the phone heard his name he asked, "Is this the stuntman?"

"Yes, this is Colin Wright. I'm calling to check on the motor home we're traveling with. Any news?"

"The radiator of the motor home your friends were traveling in boiled over. They had it towed to Pueblo. They're waiting for a rental car to be delivered. In the meantime they're waiting with the trailer."

Colin couldn't believe it. "What about their cell phone?"

"I don't know anything about that," he said. "We'll send the trooper with them now to come get you and give you a ride if you'd like."

"What mile marker are they at?" Colin waited while the man retrieved the information, giving Nikki the news while he waited for the latest. "What do you want to do?"

She looked down the road and saw a hotel sign in the distance. "We need some food. And if we don't have a place to stay tonight, we'd better be finding a hotel, preferably one with a hot tub."

Colin laughed. "You are a dreamer." He was taken off hold and made arrangements for the trooper to come meet them. At least then they wouldn't be getting all the information secondhand. When he got off the phone, Nikki reached for it.

"May I borrow it, please?"

He handed it over. "Who are you calling?"

"Mr. Chapman. A hotel would reserve a room on his credit card."

"Wait just a minute. We don't know enough details to commit to that yet. For all we know, another RV may be on the way."

"And it may just be some jalopy to pull the trailer, too. I say we act now. As you pointed out, we're not in the middle of Denver. Finding two rooms might not be as easy as it sounds."

Colin waited patiently, praying that God would bless them with an understanding sponsor. They were already behind schedule and it had only been half a day. At this rate they would never make it in eight days.

Five minutes later the trooper arrived with Sandra in the backseat. Nikki handed Colin the phone. "The phone is dead."

The trooper's eyes brightened when Nikki joined them. "Afternoon, miss. I'm Trooper Perry." He extended his hand to her, not too anxious to let go. "This is an interesting cause of yours . . ." he said with admiration.

She smiled, trying to pull her hand from his grasp. "Thank you, but it's not really mine, it's Colin's. He and the publisher came up with the details. I'm just the reporter. Why isn't Sandra getting out of the car? Is she okay?"

He lost that starry-eyed gaze when Nikki brushed him off, confirming Colin's suspicion. The trooper rushed to the car and opened Sandra's door. "Sorry," he said. "They don't open from the inside."

Colin selfishly admitted to himself that he didn't like someone who didn't even know Nikki flirting with her. Ignoring the trooper, he turned to Nikki. "Did you reach Mr. Chapman?"

"I was on hold when the low-battery signal beeped. Then it died. I don't suppose you have the charger, do you?"

"Not with me, maybe Sandra has theirs." Colin watched the trooper walk around his car after Sandra got out. "It would be too much to expect the officer to have the same kind of cell phone we do so we can recharge ours, wouldn't it?"

"Probably so." She turned to greet Sandra and saw a bag in her hand. "What's this?" Nikki asked as she gave Sandra a hug. "I was getting worried about you and Jared."

"It's a long story. Here, enjoy your lunch."

"What do we have?" Nikki said as she pulled items from the sack. She turned to Colin and smiled.

"Peanut butter and jelly sandwiches, apples and water. Eat up. Jared is waiting for the rental truck to arrive. The RV dealer insisted they need to do the work themselves, or we'd have to pay for the repairs. Jared told them they were welcome to pay the towing bill to Denver, and they reconsidered. They called the RV place in Pueblo, which was the next closest service center. We'll have to pick it up on our way through Pueblo."

"They'll have it done tomorrow morning?" Colin said between bites.

Sandra frowned. "You really think you

can make it that far by tomorrow morning? It's almost fifty miles."

"More than that because we'll have to backtrack a few miles to where we stopped riding," Nikki replied. "Which in my opinion is right here. I'm not taking another step of the relay today. I hope we can make up for lost time with a good night's sleep."

"We lost too much time today not to push for more tomorrow," Colin said with a shrug. "Any idea what's wrong with the motor home?"

"The mechanic thinks it's a broken hose, so unless there is something more major than that, they should have it ready when we get there," Sandra explained.

Colin unwrapped a second sandwich and opened the bottle of water. "I tried to call for two hours, what happened to your phone?"

"It went dead during the call to the dealer and Jared was afraid to turn any power on in the motor home to recharge it. Then he forgot the car chargers in the motor home when they pulled it away. Luckily we'd given our location so the dealer called AAA and they found us. We were able to move most of our personal belongings out of the RV and into the trailer while we waited for the trooper to arrive. He's calling around for a hotel for us. Sounds like the nearest one is in Walsenburg. Or at least the nearest one with a few luxury amenities that I thought would be appreciated after today. Namely, a hot tub to soak in."

"You read my mind," Nikki said with a smile.

By sunset they had all made it to the hotel and had eaten a steak dinner, after which they got bathing suits on and met in the hot tub to discuss alternative plans.

"How odd is it that both sets of cell phones went dead?" Sandra pondered.

"Not too strange if they were searching for a network all night. We forgot to plug ours in before we went to bed last night." Jared turned to Colin. "Did you charge yours?"

Colin shook his head. "I didn't even notice that we didn't have service at the campsite. So much for innovation. My digital had better battery life than this satellite phone."

"Ditto." Jared closed his eyes and sank down into the hot tub while his wife sat on the edge with her feet dangling in the water.

"What a day," Sandra said.

"Amen to that," the men added.

Colin laughed as he looked at Jared sprawled in the hot tub. "And you weren't even crimped onto that little itty-bitty tricycle."

Jared closed his eyes and leaned his head back against the edge. "I was busy trying to play mechanic and moving company. You should have taken the blades when I offered them."

"Hindsight is better than foresight. I think the main thing we need to change is to stay closer together. With the bicycle and kick-scooter being faster modes of transportation it shouldn't be nearly as taxing on Nikki, me, or the truck."

Jared nodded. "True, but I still don't want to plug along like that. Of course, we won't have nearly as many steep grades to deal with from here on. Maybe we should have gotten walkie-talkies instead of the cell phones."

"Anyone had experience in the Black Forest area? Will we have a problem with a signal there?"

No one answered. A few minutes later Nikki spoke up. "Why don't we call the state trooper. Maybe he'd be able to find out for us. He was quite helpful."

"Helpful? I'd call it interested. And not in 'the cause,' either. I wouldn't doubt it if he even asked for your phone number."

Nikki's jaw dropped open while Jared and

Sandra smiled quietly. "And if he did, what concern is it of yours?" she asked saucily.

Colin glanced at each of them as she watched the play of emotions on his face. "There has to be some rule against cops flirting while on duty."

Jared laughed. "You're just jealous that he got the courage to ask for her phone number before you did."

Nikki looked at Colin quickly, hopefully, but Colin didn't respond. What she hoped he'd say, she wasn't sure, but his silence cut to the quick. She couldn't help that she not only found Colin attractive, but she admired the man he was as well. Obviously he didn't share that sentiment as much as she thought.

"It's getting late," Nikki said. "If we're going to make fifty miles tomorrow, I'd better get my article written and get some sleep." She rose to get out of the hot tub.

As a child, she had loved that her family had money, but in the last five years, she'd come to resent that she'd been born with a silver spoon in her mouth. It wasn't even a matter of trusting men, it was all relationships. Her female friends had taken as much advantage of her status as anyone.

"I'm going to call it a night, too," Sandra said as she followed Nikki. "I've had enough of the heat, anyway."

"Call when you're ready to start tomorrow morning," Jared said as he wrapped his towel around his waist. "I saw a pancake house in town, thought we'd stop there and load you up with carbohydrates before the long day."

Nikki wrapped the towel around her hips and attempted to slip her waterlogged feet into her tennis shoes. She heard splashing behind her and imagined the guys laughing about anyone wanting her phone number.

She fought to maintain control of her emotions until she was in the privacy of her own room. Was it so wrong to want to be loved for who she was, without a dowry to buy a suitable husband?

"Nikki, could I talk to you?" Colin said, startling her from her personal pity party. He looked at Jared and Sandra. "Alone, if you don't mind. It'll only take a few minutes." He waved his hands, and still they hesitated.

Nikki stared at him speculatively, then turned to Sandra. "Go ahead."

"I hope that's a statement of trust." Colin's gaze swept over her face approvingly and Nikki reconsidered his brush-off just moments before.

She wanted to trust him, but the reminders of Rory kept her realistic. "You've given me no reason *not* to trust you."

"I'm sorry for what just happened. I didn't want it to sound like I'd been goaded into asking for your number, but somehow that, too, backfired. I wanted you to know my interest is sincere, not because Jared dared me." He glanced toward the doorway, where he half expected to see Jared craning around the corner to listen. "After sticking my foot in my mouth at the barbecue . . . well, I was a little cranky that day. It was a day of bitter memories that I had hoped to be able to forget by going to the party. Truth be known, if it had been any other day of the year, I'd have asked for your number then."

He could feel her eyes boring into his. "And what made you think I had money? Guilt by association?"

He shrugged, then eventually nodded. "It was totally unfair of me to . . ."

"Yes, it was," she said, a slight tremor in her voice as she tried to shed her own guilt. "It is good to know that money doesn't rule your life. Since you don't have anything to write with, I'll give you my number later." A smile teased her lips.

"I have a good memory for important details like that . . ."

She recited the number and he repeated it quietly. "Got it. So, *did* the trooper ask for your phone number?"

Nikki laughed. "Even if he had, I wouldn't have given it to him. I don't give out my home number to people I don't know," she said softly, her ice-blue eyes narrowing. "We really should call it a night. I still have an article to write, and it's going to be another challenging day tomorrow."

Colin didn't want the evening to end quite yet, but he understood. "Why don't we meet in the lobby in a few minutes? I could help you with the article."

She shook her head. "Don't worry about it. I'll get it done. After all, it would be a little challenging for you to be impartial."

"Are you impartial?" He leaned closer and lowered his voice.

"At this moment I am, but if I don't leave now, I may not be. I don't want to botch my first assignment because of distractions," she added in an equally low and husky tone.

"Such as this?" His words disappeared on her lips. He intended to keep his kiss as gentle and light as a summer breeze, until he tasted her lips — soft and delicious and slightly tart. He wanted more than anything to kiss her again. It was a dangerous game he was playing. Colin backed away.

It was a few seconds before Nikki pried her eyes open and responded. "That was more than a distraction." She blinked, then backed quickly away.

Colin smiled lazily.

Nikki shook her head and wagged her index finger. "Don't confuse me any more, Colin. How am I supposed to think, let alone write after you . . ." Her voice disappeared. She shook her head and backed her way out of the pool area. "This is a job, and you're the subject. I have to remain impartial."

"That's out the window now, huh? I just wanted you to know how much I really care for you."

She missed the door and walked into the glass next to it, stumbling. He took a step and she regained her composure, warding him off with one hand. "Don't do that again. At least not until this assignment is over."

Chapter Fourteen

Colin suspected he would regret it, but he got back into the hot tub, hoping to give them both space. He wasn't quite ready to deal with Jared's joshing, and he'd pushed Nikki as far as he dared for one day. He didn't appreciate Jared's goading, but couldn't blame his friend for his own stupidity.

He leaned his head back, closed his eyes and searched for the right words to describe the day. *Pain* immediately came to mind as he let the jetted massage work out the knots. *Confusing* was another good choice. Everything he thought was carefully planned had turned out wrong. Which brought us here, he thought, to a wonderfully relaxing hot tub. *Thank you for guiding and protecting Nikki and me from harm, Lord. Thank you for providing an equally enthusiastic and physically fit teammate. Now if you could just erase the last fifteen or so minutes, we'll be back on track.*

He closed his eyes and recalled Nikki's smile as her flaxen hair blew in the breeze from racing down the pass today. She had enjoyed the challenges as much as he had. *Keep me from temptation, Father. Nikki is different than the others, and I don't quite know what to think of that yet.*

He got out of the tub a few minutes later and dried off. It seemed too early to be going to bed since he usually worked the night shift at the radio station, but they did need to leave early in the morning.

He stopped at the candy machine and examined the many choices of salty and sweet snacks, determining that it wasn't unreasonable for his body to crave an additional dose of either after the day he'd put it through. He'd sacrifice a soda for a bag of chips and a bite of chocolate. Both were carbs, he reasoned, and he'd need the energy for the long day tomorrow. He opened his wallet and fingered a dollar bill, hesitating. *Blessed is anyone who endures temptation.*

Colin looked in both directions and even around the corner. He ran a hand over his nearly shaven head and face, calculating the strength of his willpower.

His stomach growled, and he surmised it must be almost time for his evening commute out of the city to the station. He always munched on something during the drive.

"I did pray for strength against temptation. That'll teach me to be more specific." He put his wallet away and crossed the lobby to the stairway. He set his stopwatch, pressed the start button and took off to the third floor. Twenty-five seconds flat. Not bad for someone as stiff as he had been earlier in the day. He returned to his room, slightly surprised not to find Jared there. That meant he and Sandra must have gone to Nikki and Sandra's room, which could mean Nikki could be wandering around in the hotel somewhere.

His skin felt as tight as if he'd washed up on the beach and baked in the sun. He quickly showered the chlorine off and dressed, then smoothed aloe gel over his mildly sunburned scalp, reminding himself to buy another baseball cap in the morning. His eyes still burned from the sunscreen he'd used today.

Jared hadn't returned by the time he was cleaned up, and Colin wasn't going to wait. He slipped the room key and his wallet into his shorts pocket, just in case there happened to be something he couldn't live without, he reasoned. He searched the lobby and the meeting rooms, not seeing a sign of anyone familiar. Maybe they were all visiting in the girls' room. After a quick trip back to the second floor he discovered no one was there, either. Now he was getting worried. He went back to his room and found a note that Jared and Sandra had gone to town to buy a few supplies before the stores closed. How had he missed that earlier?

And where was Nikki? He walked each floor, hoping he'd missed her somewhere. He wandered through the lobby and stopped back at the snack machine. Resisting the cola and chocolate and peanut bars, Colin gave in and bought a package of peanuts and an iced tea. Even Nikki couldn't complain too much about his selection. He'd drunk about as much sports drink as he could handle for the day.

He stepped outside to look at the sky. Not a cloud in sight and the stars looked as bright as if they'd been painted there freshly that afternoon. He walked, thinking and worrying about Nikki. Her quiet spunk reminded him of his grandmother. He smiled. Wouldn't his mother be pleased if he found someone like Nana to spend his life with?

The grounds of the Spanish-styled hotel were as elaborate and extensive as those of a high-priced resort. Twists and turns to the stucco walls created a maze of decorative rock paths. He turned away from the hotel and heard a soft sigh of frustration, followed by a woman talking. He stopped and listened to be sure someone wasn't in trouble.

"Grandfa . . ." A yippy little dog and his owners walked past just then, and Colin missed a sentence, maybe even two, of what the woman was saying. ". . . this was a mistake."

It sounded like Nikki.

"The article sounds like something written by a third-grader. Good grief, we were stuck on tricycles all day, what can you expect? I'm thinking like a grade-schooler."

Colin stepped closer, puzzled. "Nikki?"

She jumped to her feet, dropping her electronic planner and cell phone. "Colin!" She stared for a minute, then bent down to pick up the items. She lifted the phone to her ear. "I'll have to call you back with the article, Mr. Chapman."

The moonlight reflected off the tears in the corners of her eyes, and Colin's concern transferred from his own questions to her problems. "Are you okay?"

She turned away and nodded. "Fine. A little frustrated with this article, but I'll be okay."

"I didn't mean to startle you," Colin said, still reeling from her choice of words. Had he really heard her say "grandfather" and

"Mr. Chapman" in the same conversation? "You're having trouble writing the article?"

"Our entire day sounds juvenile instead of heroic."

"Heroic? No wonder you're having trouble with the article." He blurted out his feelings before he'd thought about it. "Sorry, I shouldn't have said that." They'd done nothing heroic. Not yet, anyway. If they finished the relay and raised the half million dollars he'd set as his goal they might be considered heroic. Not until then. "I'd be happy to take a look if you want me to. After all, I did promise Mr. Chapman that I would offer any professional advice that I can."

She looked away, and he made no attempt to stop looking for some sort of resemblance between Ellis and Nikki. Without looking at Colin, she handed him her handheld planner. He wanted her to tell him willingly what was going on. He was tired and he really wasn't positive of what he'd heard. It was no time to start making accusations.

He read silently, thanks to the lighted screen on the device. Nikki remained frozen, staring into the darkness, the stubborn set of her jaw giving him the impression that she was angry with him or what he'd said. He chose his words carefully this time. "If I were writing this, I'd keep it simple, so there's room to build interest day to day. This is very colorful, but by the end of the week it will sound repetitious."

"I didn't want to be here." Her voice was rough with anxiety. "And I tried to tell you this morning . . ."

"What? When?"

"On the rocks, this morning. Grandfather insisted . . ." she looked away ". . . that I do this. I didn't want to let him down."

So he had heard correctly. "You're Ellis Chapman's granddaughter?" He wanted to make sure there were no more misunderstandings. With each word he grew more irritated, even though he had suspected it from her presence at the board meeting.

She nodded. "Will you just rewrite the article, please?"

He considered her request and what ramifications there could be if he did as she asked. "Not a chance. You want this job, you're going to have to do it yourself. I'll give you suggestions, but I'm not writing it."

"I'm not a journalist. I'm a . . ."

"Dancer. I know," he snapped without thinking.

She straightened her shoulders. "Not anymore. I'm simply not a journalist. I majored in business. Ask me for a memo and I'm fine. I thought Grandfather would find me a job working in the business office. This assignment was his idea. And it was a mistake. I told him that from the beginning."

Colin gave the handheld device back to Nikki. "Fine time to play truth or consequences, isn't it? Let's go inside where we can at least see that thing to rewrite the article." He took hold of her wrist and started walking.

"I thought you weren't going to help," she said in a voice heavy with sarcasm; she sounded just like the rich girls in his past.

He should have seen it, all the signs were there. He was close to walking away, but he couldn't. He'd promised her grandfather he'd help her, and he wouldn't be able to live with himself if he didn't. "Helping you doesn't mean writing it for you." He forced himself to stop there.

It would do no good to point out that he'd been right about her all along. She was a spoiled rich girl working her way to the top of a company simply because her grandfather owned it. His brain clicked into gear, listing reasons he wouldn't fall for another rich girl as if they were numbers on a spreadsheet.

"Colin, please don't be mad at me."

While he'd been lost in his own thoughts she'd rushed ahead and stood facing him, blocking the door.

"Dogs get mad. I'm angry, but not just at you."

Tears lit her eyes again, but didn't fall. "Let me explain, please."

"Nikki, it's late. We're both tired. You have an assignment to finish before we can go to bed . . ." He stopped. "To sleep . . . in our own rooms. It's been an unbelievably long day and way too much happened. We have seven more days and three hundred miles during which you can try to explain. I'm in no mood to discuss family right now."

He waited patiently as she stared at him in silence. With no clue what was going through her head, Colin crossed his arms over his chest and counted to one hundred, anticipating her next argument. Patience wasn't a gift he'd been born with, but he was working on it. Or, better stated, God was working on Colin.

Finally she turned and opened the door.

"There's a nook off the main lobby where we can work on the article," he suggested.

Nikki paused. "Isn't there someplace more private to rip my work apart?"

"I'm not going to rip you apart," he assured her. "Tempting as that might be right now. We need to rewrite the article. That's all."

"But Colin . . ."

"Don't, Nikki. Not tonight." He glared at her, unable to stop himself. He had been a fool to go against his instincts. He ignored the moisture in her eyes. "We'll just take out the more colorful, entertaining details and keep it more about the facts. This is the first article in the series."

"You mean like your hat landing in the tree?" she said brokenly.

He met her disarming smile with one of his own, sarcastic as it might be. "Yeah, for one. And if you give them just a hint of the humor it will bring them anxiously back for more. I guarantee it."

She sat in the chair, her gaze on him. "So the 'less is more' philosophy?"

"I hope that will keep us from sounding like grade-schoolers, which was one of your comments, wasn't it?"

Nikki nodded. "How long were you standing there?"

He ignored her. "I think we'd better concentrate on the article for now. Maybe the rest of tonight will fade away like a nightmare by morning."

"We couldn't be so lucky," she muttered.

She worked on her planner and then handed it to him. “Is the lead paragraph better now?”

Colin read the first paragraph again. “It’s perfect. You have the key elements, with an interesting twist to it. Now do the same with the rest, and you’ll have it made.”

He could see her highlighting and deleting, then tapping in new words with the pencil-like stylus. He leaned closer to see what she was typing. “Sounds good. Very good.”

They worked on revisions for half an hour, their chairs touching by the time they’d finished. “It’s ready. See, I didn’t rip you or the story. Or did I?”

She shook her head. “Thank you. I’m sorry I thought you might be . . .”

“Vengeful?” He supplied the word that described the feelings he’d had at the time. “That wouldn’t have done the cause any good. But don’t think I didn’t say plenty of prayers to keep myself in line.”

She looked at him with wide eyes.

“Yeah, I’m human, too.” He forced a smile, unable to stay too angry with her. “So we’ve dealt with the consequences, how about the truth now? I’d still like to know why you’re pretending to be someone you’re not. And why you’re so upset that I found out.”

She pressed one more button on her planner and zipped it closed, then took a deep breath. "I don't think you want to hear it tonight."

"Why don't you let me decide that for myself?"

She fidgeted in her seat, waiting as a couple walked past. "I believe I figured out why Grandfather was so insistent that I take this assignment, and I don't think you'd like it much." Her cheeks turned pink. "And as for my identity, surely you should understand how impressions change when people find out you have status or money."

"That I understand." He straightened his back. "Why would your grandfather wanting you as my watchdog make . . . ?" Suddenly he had an idea. "Your grandfather is playing matchmaker."

Chapter Fifteen

Nikki's cell phone rang and she ignored it. She and Colin stared at one another in awkward silence.

"I need to go to the room and send my article." Nikki turned toward the elevator hoping he wouldn't follow. She wanted to get into the room and get to sleep before even Sandra had a chance to ask any questions about where she'd been all evening.

She felt Colin's hand on her shoulder holding her in place while he stepped in front of her. "I'm the one who asked for your phone number, Nikki, because I wanted it. Before I knew who you're related to, or that you're obviously filthy rich."

And now that he knew, she presumed he had no intentions of calling her. Her skin felt hot again. "You don't need to bother trying to use it."

"If I do call, I know that you may decide not to answer. You already know I'm not overly fond of your family money, but it can't buy love. Especially mine. And you can't possibly believe your grandfather would stoop so low as to try to pay me off.

He's a wise enough man to know better than to try to arrange any marriage for you. What really hurts is that you think I'd go along with a scheme like that . . ."

She felt as if she and Colin had known one another forever. The honest words he spoke should have incensed her, but instead the gentleness of his voice stroked her innocent emotions. "I thought Grandfather would be different from my parents," she said quietly. "I thought he would help me find a career, not try to find me a husband."

"If it helps, he never mentioned he had a gorgeous granddaughter that he wanted me to meet."

She blushed even more at his compliment. "If he had, you'd have run the other way." And you still might, she thought. "Money seems to be an issue for both of us. I want to be loved for who I am, not for my money. And you . . . don't like women with money for whatever reason."

Colin put his hands on his temples and shook his head. "I really can't get into this now, Nikki. I can admit that I like you more than I wanted to. I like that you show up at the gym in worn-out sweats instead of designer fashions. I like that you want to be loved for yourself, and that you believe in helping others . . ." Colin stopped talking.

Another guest walked past them to the elevator and pressed the button, the delay interrupting Colin.

Nikki sensed she was on the verge of an emotional letdown, and hoped she'd be able to avoid another crash into depression when this relay was over. She hadn't meant to let herself feel anything for Colin, but when all of her initial opinions of his arrogance and ego had gone up in flames, so had her resolve. Suddenly she realized why her first article had been so difficult. Emotion had taken over. She had an incredible crush on Colin Wright.

What was not to like about him? He was more than attractive, he was gorgeous, in a definitely manly way. His almost-shaven head gave him a worldly sophisticated appeal. Except for the easy smile and wholesome look to his face he looked a little like Sean Connery. Colin enjoyed life and shared that joy with others. Not many men would be caught dead riding a tricycle on a neighborhood street let alone a public highway.

Nikki felt a frantic need to get away from him. She didn't want him to see the pain when he tried to let her down easily. They had no choice but to finish this assignment, and it could be very awkward. However, if she got into the elevator with the other guest, it would only make the inevitable more difficult. They might as well talk it out now.

She nodded toward the front doors and started outside. "Let's take a walk."

He shook his head. "Not tonight."

"Please, let me explain."

Once they'd walked into the chilly mountain air, they were encased in darkness. Nikki sat on the corner of a bench at the far edge of the gardens where they could see if anyone was coming.

"Colin, I didn't mean to deceive you, but I know it appears that way. All of my life, I've never known if friends liked me because of who I was, or because I had money. When I came to Denver I didn't want to be Ellis and Naomi Chapman's granddaughter. I just wanted to be Nikki Post, whoever that is."

Colin was quiet for a minute. "I understand that part, Nikki. Really. It's hard to find someone who is sincere and not just out for a brush with the good life."

She nodded. She'd never thought about him having the same insecurities when it came to relationships, because she'd only been worried about protecting herself. "I didn't think of it that way before."

Colin leaned on the retaining wall across from her and crossed his strong arms over his chest. "When I met you at Jared and Sandra's there was an air of elegance that set off warning signals inside me. You didn't have to say a word. Your clothes didn't tip me off. Definitely wasn't your car. Maybe it was that all those pieces of you didn't fit together." His voice seemed even deeper when he was trying to be quiet. "Yet in the few weeks we have spent together preparing for this relay, I convinced myself that you weren't the type to lie."

He'd trusted her and she'd done exactly what he'd expected. "I'm sorry, Colin." Nikki closed her eyes and squeezed the tears back.

"I wanted to think that I had been completely off base and unfair to make judgments based upon my own track record. I prayed that this time it would be different. I wanted so badly for you to be the exception to the rule. And I can't begin to tell you how disappointed I am right now." He sat next to her and put his elbows on his knees, pressing the palms of his hands into his temples. "Right now I'm drowning in confusion."

"Colin, we don't need to worry about this anymore . . ."

"Maybe *you* don't, but it's too late for me. When that trooper started flirting with you I wanted to deck him, and I'm not that type. I never even hit my own brother when we got into tussles as kids."

She couldn't keep back the sob of emotion. No one had ever told her he'd been jealous over her before. "I'm flattered," she whispered. "And I'm so sorry."

"And feeling that much for you is terrifying to me, Nikki. Love isn't supposed to be jealous."

"Love isn't perfect, either. Besides, it's a little soon for love." She expected him to jump in to correct himself. "Isn't it?"

He shrugged. "Probably, but I don't know. Which is why this is so confusing. You make this so easy and yet so difficult. I made a lot of changes in my life this year. I felt God leading me away from the comforts of my high-profile job to this small Christian radio station. I couldn't get enough time studying His word. And when I was asked to join the team at WWJD radio, I knew it had to be God's plan. Then this project came to light, and I loved the idea of doing something out of the ordinary.

"Everyone warned me that there would be opposition because of the controversy surrounding the homeless projects. Then

Mr. Chapman approached me about it and he threw in a few more unexpected steps. Never once did I hesitate.

"And when I saw you at that board meeting, I couldn't decide whether to be insulted or thrilled."

Nikki felt the passion people described as God's spirit emanating from Colin and it frightened her. She might not know as much about God as she should, but she knew better than to discount His power. She was afraid of being to blame for causing Colin to falter, personally or professionally. "I'm so sorry, Colin. I don't even know what to say. What can I do to fix the problem?" She admired him too much to cause him any hurt or pain. "Would it help if I just rode with Sandra and Jared?"

He looked at her and laughed. "No, that wouldn't solve anything."

"Maybe if I acted more like a selfish rich girl . . ."

"Nikki, Nikki, Nikki. Don't you dare." She felt goose bumps spread up her arms at the warmth of his hand holding hers. "Don't you even think of being anyone but yourself. That's the woman I'm attracted to, and if God wants us together, He'll lead us through that journey . . . if we trust Him to do so."

She pulled her hand from his.

"What's wrong?"

She had no more control and the tears flowed.

"Nikki, what did I say?"

"I think there's been a big misunderstanding." Her head began spinning. "I don't . . ." That wasn't it. She did believe in God. But Colin's faith was obviously different than hers. "I'm not so sure . . ." She closed her eyes and struggled to express herself. To find the right words.

"Not sure of what?"

She shook her head. "I don't . . ." she inhaled deeply and let it out, desperate to regain control ". . . know . . ." Nikki glanced quickly at Colin and turned away. "I don't know that you should be feeling anything for me, Colin."

"I don't think I have any choice."

Nikki put her finger on his lips to quiet him. "I need to finish explaining to you, please."

He kissed her finger and nodded. "Go ahead."

"My religious training is very different from yours."

He nodded and waited while she explained that her parents had only taken their family to church two or three times a year.

"Have you ever heard about God's love and been offered salvation?" Colin lifted her chin and brushed away the tears.

She blinked, bringing his face into focus. He made no attempt to release her from the question. "I know Jesus died for our sins because He loved us. And I know I should go to church more, but the message is always the same." She paraphrased the miracle of Jesus Christ's birth and resurrection as the sermons she'd heard at each service she'd attended in her childhood.

"The amazing thing about God is that He never gives up on bringing His children into His fold, Nikki. He meets each one of us at the level we're at. I read the Bible as a child and understood it from a child's perspective. And those same passages still hold lessons for me, no matter what I'm going through. The Bible is a timeless book, written so we can hear God's word as clearly now as our ancestors did thousands of years ago."

"But I don't hear Him like you seem to. He didn't tell me to do this relay or help the homeless . . ." She could see the understanding in his eyes and felt oddly at ease showing her ignorance. It was no longer frightening to let him into her heart. "I don't understand what you mean by God talking to you."

"That takes time. Some Christians never do 'hear' God's voice. Some feel it, as if the worry is lifted away after they hand a problem to God. He speaks to some through scriptures that relate to where we are in life. And others see God's prayers answered, from opened doors of opportunity to people who come into and out of their lives. Finding out that my fiancée's and my goals and priorities were in different places hurt at the time, but I was eventually able to see that God had been trying to tell me Bev wasn't His intended mate for me. She wouldn't have been caught dead doing a stunt with me, even if it helped ten thousand homeless families."

Nikki wondered if God had been as busy in her life, and if she had just never recognized His helping hand, or if He had been simply waiting and watching all of her mistakes.

"God loves you, Nikki. He wants you to know the depth of His love for you. Maybe He brought you here this week to experience that firsthand. Without God as my anchor, I wouldn't be here at all. I'd have given up on the project long ago, but when the committee put God at the helm, every roadblock seemed to disappear."

She longed to understand the depth of

Colin's faith, yet didn't know what to ask for or how to begin. "I don't want to interfere with God's work for you, Colin."

"And what if you are part of God's plan, Nikki? I don't know what is coming, but I trust Him to show me the way. I looked out over the plains from the top of the pass this morning and could see where we are going. I have a map that shows me the different roads we can take. And even with a map, I can't get anywhere without trusting God to take care of me, of us. And you can see how He did that. We were sore and He found us a hot tub to ease the pain. We lost our shelter, and He more than provided for us. We were tired, and He sent an eagle to give us hope."

She looked at him, puzzled by his analogy. "How?"

"In Isaiah, God shows His ultimate power. He strips Isaiah of everything, and finally, He gives strength to the weary and increases the power of the weak. And He goes on to promise that those who hope in the Lord will renew their strength. They will soar on wings like eagles without growing weary or faint."

"You've memorized the Bible?"

His smile broadened. "Only parts of it. That way I take the hope of God with me at all times."

"How do you know what to memorize?"

"I suppose that's different for everyone. If I find a passage that really helps me through a rough time, I dog-ear it in my Bible and go back to it often, until I eventually memorize it. Others I memorize as part of a study I'm doing. It's amazing how His word returns to comfort me in times of need."

"I see why Grandfather is trying to bring us together, Colin. He obviously thinks a lot of you. Still, he shouldn't interfere like this."

"I'm flattered," he said with a big smile. "And I hope you realize he sometimes interferes with your life because he loves you and wants to see you happy, just like God wants the best for His children."

But I don't feel like God's child, she thought. And what was worse, she didn't know how to become one.

Chapter Sixteen

Colin dragged himself to the gardens early the next morning, kicking himself for letting down his guard to Nikki.

He had made sure she made it safely to her room then gone to his and Jared's room, expecting sleep to come easily. The lights had been out. Jared had already fallen asleep, for which Colin was eternally grateful because he didn't want to talk to anyone about Nikki until he figured out just how he felt.

So he'd tossed and turned, thinking about Ellis Chapman's granddaughter most of the night. By morning, he couldn't think any more. Carrying his Bible, he found a quiet place in the gardens to have a talk with God. He read Isaiah 40 in its entirety, finding comfort and direction for the day ahead. He returned to verse three.

> In the wilderness prepare the way of the Lord, make straight in the desert a highway for our God. Every valley shall be lifted up and every mountain and hill shall be made low, the uneven ground shall become level, and the rough

places a plain. And the glory of the Lord shall be revealed, and all flesh shall see it together, for the mouth of the Lord has spoken.

Colin closed his eyes and prayed. For the relay. For the homeless. And for his feelings for Nikki.

A few minutes later the four were seated in the booth at the restaurant planning out the day. Jared and Sandra had claimed one side, leaving him and Nikki to share the other half of the booth. A quick glance told him Nikki had slept as little as he had. She pressed herself against the wall, leaving as much space between them as possible.

Colin could see the suspicion in Jared and Sandra's eyes. They were about to rupture with curiosity. "How many miles to Pueblo?" he said, trying to make conversation.

Sandra looked at Nikki, who was typing away on her planner, and raised her eyebrows.

"Fifty-one from where you stopped yesterday to the campground," Jared said with a smile, elbowing Sandra.

Nikki started to say something and stopped, edging away as if Colin had fleas. That hurt worse than sliding into home base for the winning run and being called out.

"And if we don't make it all the way it will put us half a day behind, right?" Colin said, struggling to steer the conversation and his mind away from Nikki. He wanted more than anything to tell her they would work through the confusion of last night, but they didn't need more pressure and complications.

Jared pulled out the map and confirmed the route for the day. He looked from Colin to Nikki. "How late were you two up last night?"

Nikki shrugged. "I sent the article to the pressroom at ten, so it wasn't so late. By the way, Gary hopes that the home owners are going to back down on their fight to keep the shelter out. The shopping mall they wanted to build on that lot wanted too many perks and they don't act like they will go through with it if they have to pay," she read, then looked up from her Palm. "Oh, sorry, I was just checking my e-mail. Still, it's great news!"

Laughter seemed to help ease the tension. "That's great," Jared said.

Colin nodded. "Yeah, hope it works out. That seems like a good location for the families." He took a bite of toast, then looked at Jared. "It would have been nice if you'd told us you were going shopping last night, I'd have added a few things to the list," he said.

"You neither one look as if you had more than fifteen minutes of sleep as it is," Sandra teased. "You could have done your own shopping, as tired as you look."

Colin ignored the comment and, scribbling on a napkin, came up with a list of supplies he and Nikki wanted for today. "I'll carry a backpack. Is there anything else we need to take this time?" He held the list out for Nikki to read.

"Sunscreen," Nikki added. "You obviously need it."

"It gets in my eyes when I sweat," he complained.

"We found hats and bought two for each of you. I think you'd better keep an extra with you today." Sandra reached into a plastic grocery sack and pulled out the hats and a bandana. "A do-rag, just as a backup."

Everyone, including Nikki, laughed.

"Smart aleck." Colin folded the bandana into a triangle and draped it over his forehead, struggling to tie it behind his head. "What about cell phones?"

"Walkie-talkies. One for you and one for us." Sandra said as she pulled walkie-talkies from the bag. "And extra batteries. They have a five-mile range, so that should get us by until we get our phone chargers from the motor home."

Colin gave up on the bandana and set it on the table. "You found energy bars?"

"No, but they had some granola bars. You'll have to survive on those."

Colin motioned for another cup of coffee, ignoring the looks Nikki and Sandra gave him. "I don't want to hear one word. With fifty miles ahead of us, I'm going to need all the help I can get."

"You're going to be the one to pay the price," Sandra scolded. "Pack another bottle of water, and be sure you drink it."

He saluted Sandra. "Yes, ma'am." After they'd finished breakfast, Colin went to the hotel kitchen to get the food that had been refrigerated for them, then they loaded the truck and headed back to the point where they had stopped the day before.

"We're starting on the kick-scooters today, right?" It was only the second thing Nikki had said this morning.

Jared answered her question, suggesting they ride two miles on the scooters then ten on the bicycles, then back and forth until they'd completed the fifty-some miles. "I don't want you cramping up like you did yesterday. And take more water breaks. It's supposed to be in the nineties this afternoon."

"What's for lunch?" Colin asked.

"We just ate!" His three teammates bemoaned their full stomachs and he never did get an answer.

Once they reached the abandoned gas station Jared pulled into the shade and everyone climbed out. "There's our eagle, Nikki." He pointed to the bird circling over the mountain.

"With a little luck, he'll follow us all the way to Pueblo," she replied. "If you'll get the scooters out, I'll add the food to our packs."

Nikki climbed back into the truck and opened the cooler, leaving him no room to help. He and Jared unlocked the trailer and dug through the luggage and supplies until they reached the scooters. "So what happened with Nikki last night?" Jared asked. "We could cut the ice between you two with a hacksaw." Jared handed him one of the scooters and turned to release the other from the bungee cord.

Colin didn't know how much they knew about Nikki, and didn't have time to completely explain. Besides that, he wanted more time to make sure things were smoothed over with her before he said anything to anyone. "We talked about God and family, mostly. I think we're both just tired from yesterday."

Jared gave him a look of disbelief that Colin returned with a tight-lipped smile.

"Whatever," Jared groaned. "Just pace yourselves a little better today. Variety is the spice of life you know."

Colin eased a scooter over each shoulder and headed to the truck. "You'll meet us two miles up the road, right? And don't forget to tie the Pedestrians Ahead sign on the trailer before you leave."

"We'll be there. Set your walkie-talkie on channel seven."

"It's in my pack," Colin said as he admired Nikki. Even tired she was a sight for sore eyes. Her silky hair was loose today, under a Colorado Rockies cap. Despite the predicted heat, she wore athletic pants with the legs pulled up to her knees and a long-sleeved T-shirt. He handed her a scooter, setting it on the ground beside her. "Are you ready?"

Nikki nodded. "Whenever you are. Would you like me to tie the bandana for you?"

Her offer caught him off guard, and he dug the scarf out of his backpack. "Sure. It beats sunscreen in the eyes. When you're done, why don't we start the day right," he suggested as she tied the bandana around his head. "Jared?"

His friend popped his head out of the trailer. "Did you call me?" He smiled at Colin's biker image. "Hey, nice look."

Sandra waved for him to join them. "We're going to pray." Jared jogged to the circle and they wrapped arms around one another's shoulders and bowed their heads. Sandra started and when she paused, Jared asked for God's blessing on the relay, for safety and stamina for Nikki and Colin. He stopped and the silence lingered. Finally Colin wrapped it up with a request that each of them would feel His presence and guidance every step of the way. Without hesitation, they all said "Amen."

Jared and Sandra moved away, and, not wanting to embarrass Nikki, Colin stepped close and whispered in her ear, "Are you okay?"

She turned suddenly and nodded.

"You're awfully quiet," he said softly.

She glanced over her shoulder. "Sandra woke me up with a hundred and one questions, which I had no answers for. Then there was that prayer. I guess I feel even more out of place this morning."

"Everything feels a little out of sorts this morning." He considered giving her a quick hug, but figured that would only complicate matters. "Sorry if I added to the difficulty of the morning with the prayer. I think it's important the entire team be on the same page. Especially since it's going to be such a challenging day."

"You really think it will help?" Her eyes begged for someone to put her trust in.

"He'll prove it to you. We have fifty miles to cover, little to no sleep to run on — at least if you slept half as poorly as I did. And with a record-setting temperature on the forecast, I'd say His power will be put to the test." He reached out for her scooter and handed it to her. "God will take care of us." He touched the bandana. "Thank you, by the way."

She shrugged. "It's all part of the teamwork. The last thing we need is you collapsing from a sunburn because you're too stubborn to wear sunscreen." She adjusted her waist pack and put her sunglasses on.

If he didn't know better, he'd almost think she actually cared if he did collapse. After last night, he wouldn't have blamed her for walking away altogether.

"You go first today. I'll follow," she said.

"Ladies first, unless you'd like me to break the trail for you?"

"You think I'm not capable?" She shifted her weight to the scooter and took off. The thing he liked the most about Nikki was her competitiveness.

"I knew I could get you," he hollered, not at all sure she could hear him. About fifteen minutes later, Sandra and Jared beeped the horn and slowly passed them.

"How's it going?" Sandra leaned out the window and waited for Colin's reply.

"We're making record time." Nikki hadn't slowed down until they'd come to a long, grueling hill. It was taxing both of them.

"Meet you in another mile and a quarter," she yelled as Jared accelerated. Colin looked over his shoulder to see why they'd sped up so quickly, shocked to see two eighteen-wheelers, side by side, coming down the hill. "Get over, Nikki!"

Colin dropped the scooter's handlebars and ran, tackling her just as the semis rumbled past. The draft from the trucks tossed them into the sagebrush like rag dolls. Having rolled to the bottom of the ditch like a log, Colin untangled himself from Nikki and pushed himself to one side. He leaned back, examining her. "You hurt?"

The surprise on her face was frightening. "I don't think so. Are you?"

He pulled a twig from her hair and looked for her cap. "I'm sorry, I thought the trucks were closer."

"They felt plenty close to me." She sat up

and looked at him. "Thanks for the save."

Colin took a deep breath and let it out, wondering if he'd overreacted. They might have been blown over had they both stayed on the scooters, but he wasn't so sure they'd have been hurt. He took another deep breath and brushed the dirt and weeds from his clothes, then rested his head in his hands.

"Colin?" Nikki knelt in front of him. "Colin. Are you okay?"

He nodded, struggling not to think about what could have happened. He looked behind them to his discarded scooter lying in the ditch. Hers was nowhere in sight.

"Here, drink some water." She handed him a bottle.

He pushed it away. "Nikki, where's your scooter?"

"I don't care. You're pale as a ghost and your breathing sounds funny. Drink." She offered it again, and he took it, just to make her happy.

She didn't understand, he thought. He guzzled half the bottle and set it aside, then took her face in his hands. "I'm sorry I hurt you, Nikki . . ."

"I'm fine." She rocked back on her heels and out of his grasp, brushing the dust from her clothes.

Colin shook his head. "I mean last night, and at the barbecue . . ." He poured the cold water over his head, shook it off then took another drink. "And just now, I don't know . . . I couldn't imagine letting you get hurt."

Nikki inched closer. "I'm okay, Colin. As you said, God's watching over us. I felt Him, when you dove at me, and we just landed in these weeds instead of wrapped around the fence post like my scooter." She pointed toward the field.

He stared at her scooter in shock. "Oh, Nikki. I could have lost you."

Chapter Seventeen

Nikki reeled with emotion. Surely Colin didn't mean that the way it sounded. He was upset. They both were. "You couldn't be so lucky. I'm right here."

"Don't even say such a thing." He stared at her in disbelief. "Why would you even think I'd consider it lucky if you had been hurt?" He didn't wait for her to think, let alone reply. He took her into his arms and held her close. "Don't ever think that again, Nikki. It's absolutely not true."

"I was joking," she said defensively. "Don't worry, I'm really okay. I'm better than okay."

Colin fingered a loose tendril of hair and brushed it off her cheek. "You'd better be. After all, I made a promise to your grandfather, and I plan to keep up my end of the deal."

It was as if he'd thrown a bucket of ice over her head. "Well, I'll be sure he knows you haven't let him down." She turned away and knelt down to get her baseball cap.

Colin beat her to it. "Nikki, don't start

imagining things. I didn't mean that the way it sounded."

"Are you sure of that, Colin? After all, you have a lot riding on this relay. And I am the one person who could stand in the way of you getting what you want, aren't I?" She pushed him away and marched to the fence post that had been broken in half by a flying scooter. "You'd better get going. I certainly don't want to be the one to slow you down. I'll catch up." From the corner of her eye she saw him toss her cap to the ground and follow her.

Silently he wrestled the bent scooter off the rotted fence post and started walking along the ditch. "There's a difference in doing something for my own profit and doing it for someone else." He stopped and glared at her. "And don't think for a minute that you can keep me from finishing on time."

She shook her head. "I have no intention of trying."

He continued walking. Nikki picked up his scooter and walked at her own pace. She was not about to push her way past him now. A hot gust of wind blew a brown curtain of dirt from west to east across the plains, giving Colin reason to question his wisdom in doing this stunt. And he could be sure Jared would ask as well.

They topped the next hill and saw the pickup and trailer sitting along the shoulder of the highway with the emergency lights blinking. Colin coughed, almost like a tickle in the throat at first, then it became deeper. Before he could reach Jared, Colin pulled the water from his bag and guzzled the remainder of the bottle to clear his throat.

Two bicycles were perched alongside the trailer. Sandra and Jared were sitting in the ditch waiting, as if nothing had happened. Colin swung the mangled scooter from his shoulder and set it on the ground with a thud.

Jared walked circles around it as if it were going to jump back to life. "I'm assuming neither of you were on this when that happened." He raised an eyebrow and glanced at Nikki as she arrived with the undamaged scooter. "So, what happened?"

Colin had gone directly to the trailer and climbed inside. Nikki watched and waited. The bikes were already out and he hadn't taken the scooters inside with him. What was he doing?

"Nikki? Are things going okay?" Sandra asked. She could hear Colin clearing his throat again, and then a small cough.

"Yeah, we just had a close call with those

semis that were following you." She glanced nervously at the trailer again. "Just as we were caught in the trucks' draft, Colin knocked me off the scooter and we landed in the ditch. I didn't think we were that close to the road, but somehow the scooter ended up wrapped around a fence post."

"This is ridiculous," Jared grumbled. "Colin! You have to call this off!"

Colin stepped out of the trailer with a fresh bottle of water. "Not a chance. You think it's any safer for the homeless?" He twisted the top from the bottle, dragging in a deep breath before he chugged the contents.

"They're not living along the highway, getting blown away by eighteen-wheelers going seventy miles an hour."

"You haven't seen the box homes under the viaducts lately, have you? Having all of our plans fall to pieces and our camper ripped from under our feet yesterday gave me a taste of how they must feel. And this is a temporary situation. Imagine their panic when they don't have a clue whether they will have a bed to sleep in that night or food for their families that week." He paused to glare at Jared, then continued on to the bicycles. "I don't care if the rest of you want to go home, but I'm sticking it out."

He put his helmet on, climbed onto the bicycle and took off without another word.

"I'll see you in a few miles," Nikki said as she exchanged her cap for the helmet and followed him.

They rode in relative silence as wind and dust made the ride not only hot but miserable. The only sign of life was a string of willows along the dried-up creek bed that wound through the golden prairie. Tumbleweeds had tangled with and lost to the barbed-wire fences. Side roads were few and far between.

Colin had been coughing off and on, but hadn't said much at all. It wasn't like him. Even though he was angry with her, he was unusually quiet.

She noticed a pile of what looked like chunky black rocks in the middle of the flat field. "What is that?"

"Huerfano Butte," he said in a gruff voice.

He didn't sound good. He sounded as though he was catching a cold, but that made no sense. "Need some water?"

He shook his head. "At the top of the hill we'll stop for a break and have a snack." Their progress slowed considerably as they looked ahead. It was a long, gradual incline. Colin leaned forward on his cycle, shifted to a lower gear, and started coughing again.

She knew Colin would get cranky if she kept bothering him about his health, but she wanted some way to measure how he was feeling. "I wish this wind would die down, or at least blow at our backs and give us some help."

"Jesus told his disciples that they could move mountains if they only had faith the size of a mustard seed. You have that, don't you?"

"I don't need the mountains moved, I just want the wind and dust to stop."

"You know who to ask about that, and it wouldn't be me."

Ask God to change the wind? Colin *was* tired. "I think you need to take a few minutes to rest, Colin."

"I think I need a few *hours* of rest. And so do you, but that's a long ways off. I'm not stopping until I get to Pueblo," he yelled over his shoulder, then coughed a couple of times. "Once we make it to the top here, we have a nice long downslope into town. We've climbed two thousand feet in elevation since breakfast. Now we're going to have a break for a day. Tomorrow we'll have another . . ."

His voice was lost in the wind. She pushed harder to get closer so she could hear Colin, surprised by his heavy breathing. She had to admit, this workout beat anything she'd done at the gym, but he hadn't shown any sign of problems when they trained in the mountains. Still, the wind today made a ten-mile run feel like child's play. "Aren't you tired?"

"Thanks to you I am."

"Me?"

"It's your fault I didn't get any sleep last night," Colin teased. He slowed as they went around the huge curve and reached the peak, pulling to a stop. He pulled his bicycle off the highway and into the shade of a bluff.

Nikki removed her helmet and pulled her hair atop her head, turning her back to the dirt blowing off the mountains. She stretched to one side, then the other, admiring the golden view of the plains. A herd of cattle stood with their backs to the wind also. She lunged backwards to keep her muscles from tightening up, using the uneven ground to her benefit to deepen the stretch. "You need to stretch, Colin."

Rather than standing up, he folded himself in half and rested his elbows on his knees, appearing to have collapsed. "There. I'll even pull my toes toward my body."

She shook her head, trying to hide her

smile. Why, when he annoyed her so, did she still want to know him better? They'd grown up with totally different perspectives on life and living. He was far more interested in faith than she, and yet . . .

"Come sit down out of the sun and wind — rest a minute. We can't stop for long." His sentence ended in a tight cough, and he opened the backpack and began searching inside. "Let me get you a granola bar."

Nikki pulled her long-sleeved shirt off while he dug through the pack. Thankful that she had dressed in layers, she spread the pink shirt over the clay-colored rocks to keep its sweaty dampness from staining her white tank top. Colin handed her a water, and turned his head in surprise.

"You just now getting hot? Why were you wearing that long-sleeved T-shirt if you had another top on?"

"I wore the long sleeves because the arm pads cut into my skin and I thought blading was on the schedule today. I didn't have time to think, let alone change at our last stop."

He gave an approving smile. "Sorry about the confusion."

She poured some of the water onto the long-sleeved shirt and then washed her face and neck. She drank the rest.

Their walkie-talkie buzzed and she heard Colin say, "Hey, we're on top of the ridge above Colorado City and Rye turnoff. If you're through napping, you can stop by and give us a bottle of sports drink. I think we could use some electrolytes." He paused, polishing off his bottle of water while he listened. "I knew it was too good to be true. I guess we'd better start planning out an alternative. See you in a few minutes."

"What's wrong now?"

"The motor home has some major problems. They won't have it ready for us to use this week." He closed his eyes and reclined, covering his eyes with his cap.

"I'm sure Grandfather can arrange for another . . ."

He cut her off. "I think it would be easier just to find a hotel every day. Some days will be cut a little shorter, but the hotels won't cost much more than gasoline for that tank. I can't believe we've had such problems already," Colin mumbled.

"Don't be so hard on yourself, Colin." She pulled a tube of moisturizing lip gloss from her waist pack and applied it to her parched lips.

He shook his head, muttering under the bill of his cap. " 'Fear not, for I am with you.

Do not get discouraged. The Lord is with us. . . .' " He took another deep breath and a drink of water, and sat up to look at Nikki. "The Lord started this for a reason, and whatever that is, He'll get us through to the finish. Maybe it's not so much about the speed as it is endurance. After all, the homeless don't get the luxury of a hotel room when things don't work out as planned."

Nikki's eyes opened wide. "You're not suggesting we sleep out here without any supplies . . ." The thought sent a chill up her spine. She'd watched enough reality television shows to know some people would do anything for attention. Maybe Colin was one of them.

"Those less fortunate do it."

"Without a tent or sleeping bags, or anything? You can't . . ." She gave him a look of disgust that she was sure had "spoiled rich girl" echoing in his ears.

He started laughing. "Gotcha . . ." He shook his head. "We're not close enough to campgrounds to do that, and I'm not adding miles on to try it, though it was considered on our original plan until CDOT took so long to get things approved." He glanced at her. "Hey, do you happen to have some non-shiny lip stuff I could borrow?"

Was he teasing her again? "I have some,

but I don't share my lip gloss. That's like sharing a toothbrush."

He laughed. "I didn't ask to lick it or eat it, I just want to put a little on my lips. But I guess I'll have Jared pick up some for me, since you don't share."

She shrugged. "I'm sorry. It's just so . . . unsanitary. But if you want it, I'll buy another when we get to town. You can have this one." She started to dig it out again.

He held up his hand. "No, that's okay. Nice to know where you stand on that issue before I get any ideas. Besides, I don't want my lips to look as . . . um, shiny as yours, anyway." He rambled on. His cough had disappeared, she realized, and he was talking fine, a mile a minute, in fact. He must have had a tickle in his throat from the dry, dusty air. He was still complaining about her not sharing her lip gloss.

Nikki closed her eyes and tried to tune him out. "I'm not listening to any more razzing about my personal hygiene."

He laughed, the soft rumble bouncing off the rock wall behind them and rolling out onto the pasture. "So," he said, "if I were to ask you for a kiss, you'd say no, because it's unsanitary, huh?"

She opened her eyes and looked at him. He seemed very pleased with himself for surprising her. When she looked at it that way, her argument with the lip gloss was rather ridiculous, which she was sure he'd point out next. "You'd have to ask to get an answer."

"Well, I would, but my lips are all chapped and dry and dusty, and I'd want our kiss to be a little more memorable, since we have a golden view of forever in front of us."

She didn't know how to answer. "I thought we'd agreed to forget the whole issue."

"Then I realized just how special it is for God to introduce me to a woman who doesn't need or want my money, who will go through this for her family and people she doesn't even know."

She rolled her eyes and shook her head as she stood and shook out her shirt. "You must be hallucinating from the heat. I'm just here to watch out for my grandfather's interests, remember? Don't let your imagination run away with you, Colin. I'm still the selfish rich girl that you'd love to hate."

He grabbed her ankle. "Sit down, Nikki."

Her heart stopped at his serious tone. She sat next to him.

"I reconsidered, and wonder if God is telling me not to be so judgmental, especially when He's blessed me by introducing me to a woman who enjoys His outdoors as much as I do. I've been just as wrong as anyone in this."

"Don't tease me, Colin. I don't want instant gratification or I would have . . ."

"Ditto," he said, motioning for her to meet him halfway.

Colin edged closer, wiping his face clean just as Sandra and Jared beeped the horn, kicking dirt up as they pulled off the highway.

The two turned away, protecting themselves from flying debris. Colin chuckled. "One of these days I'm going to get the timing right — on everything."

Chapter Eighteen

They pulled into Pueblo late that afternoon and went directly to the RV shop to get the rest of their belongings out of the motor home before they moved on. Afterward they stopped for dinner and bought a few necessities before turning in.

Colin woke the next morning refreshed and ready to go. Since they were going to be traveling on city streets and smaller highways, he was ever thankful for the rest. They didn't need another mishap like yesterday's.

"Seems you and Nikki settled whatever was bothering you yesterday at breakfast," Jared said as he packed his bag.

"It's a start," Colin answered, then started his electric razor and trimmed his head and face close.

"I was right about her, wasn't I?" Jared stacked their belongings next to the door.

Colin didn't want to make any guesses how serious this could get yet. "Well," he said, "she won't be after *my* money, that's for sure. And we do have a lot in common."

"What do you mean, she won't be after your money?"

"Ellis Chapman is her grandfather."

"You're kidding? But . . . ?" He shook his head. "What's with the act? The old car? The job?"

He shrugged. "It's a long story." He hadn't stopped to make sense of everything yet. "She doesn't seem as focused on the niceties of life as Bev, but I'm in no hurry to jump to any more conclusions. Before I even consider letting it get serious I need to find out where she stands on a few of those issues Bev and I didn't discuss."

The thought of his ex-girlfriend left him somber. She'd come into his life and changed things in his apartment so subtly he hadn't even noticed. Where he'd once had homemade gifts from his niece and nephews he now had expensive art and sculptures. He hadn't wanted to keep the gifts when they broke up, but she had insisted his apartment needed it more than she did. He'd meant to find someone who would appreciate them, but hadn't gotten around to it. Now he realized he hadn't wanted to totally let go of the objects because they gave him a constant reminder of the anger and pain. Finally he was more than ready to let all of that go.

Nikki and Colin started the day on the

pogo sticks, jumping their way through downtown during rush hour. They both wore their T-shirts advertising the toll-free number to donate to the Back on Track Relay and had received a fair share of honks and supportive cheers.

The tightness in Colin's chest had subsided with the full night of sleep, but the strong smell from the steel mills spelled trouble if he didn't get out of the city quickly. The coughing had subsided, and Colin said a prayer of thanks in his morning devotions and asked for an extra measure of protection from illness and injury in the coming days.

He stopped at the red light and jumped off the stick. "Nikki," he said, surprised by a crowd across the street, "what would you think of taking time off to go to church in Colorado Springs tomorrow morning?"

She stretched one leg, then the other, nodding at a few people as they waited for the light to turn green. "I can't go to church in my sweats."

"Sure we can. I have a friend who asked if we'd stop in. He knows we're not going to be dressed up. I think the break would be good for us . . . ."

The light turned green and Nikki got back on the pogo stick without answering. Colin hoped that he was right to push now, that the Lord had planted a seed of faith in Nikki, one that could grow and flourish. It was easy to share his faith over the wires to listeners who had made the choice to turn to WWJD radio. It wasn't even difficult to witness to strangers, but it terrified him to think that he wouldn't be able to reach someone he cared so much about.

What would he do if Nikki didn't pursue a deeper fellowship with God? And if she took that step, how could he be sure her commitment was from the heart, for the right reasons? He hadn't worried this much about anything since he'd signed the contract to play professional ball.

"Colin!" The horn beeped, and Sandra waved. "Colin, it's a red light. You missed the turn." He jumped off the pogo stick and watched as traffic streamed down Abriendo Avenue.

"What were you doing?" Nikki asked.

"Just thinking. A little too much, I guess." And not trusting, he thought, scolding himself.

She motioned to the sky. "Looks like we're in for another windy day."

He looked up, studying the light wispy clouds that held no moisture, but came before a storm front. That wasn't good news. Turning to Nikki, he asked, "You want to take a break and change to Rollerblades? I've about had it with this kangaroo imitation."

"Sounds like a winner. I have to admit, I'm liking these alternative methods of transportation less and less each day. It makes me much more thankful for what I have, even if it is a beat-up jalopy." Nikki's smile brightened his mood. He needed that.

He pulled out the lip balm he'd bought the night before and swiped it onto his lips, then put it away. If only it were so easy to let go of problems, he realized. He had spent too much time worrying about what was going to happen between him and Nikki. It was long past time to pass the problem onto a higher power. Colin had vowed to let God take the lead on his love life after his broken engagement, and he realized the problem was that he'd tried to take control again.

Colin motioned for Jared to pull over and they traded the pogo sticks for Rollerblades. He felt much more at home wearing wheels than hopping around on a stick. When the truck stopped, Sandra and Jared jumped down, laughing so hard there were tears rolling down their faces.

"What's the joke?"

Sandra pointed to her lips. "It's not your color."

Colin looked at Jared, who was puckering his lips for a big exaggerated cartoon smooch. "What has gotten into you?"

Nikki pogo-sticked in behind Colin, unable to contain her soft laugh. "What's so funny?" she asked.

"What are you laughing at?" Colin insisted. He turned to Nikki, shrugging his shoulders. Nikki's blue eyes doubled in size.

"Oh!" Immediately she, too, started laughing so hard she almost wept. "Look in the mirror, Colin."

If he hadn't been so shocked to see bright red lips on his own face, he too would have seen the same humor they did. "Who switched lip balms with me?"

"I think you did that to yourself, it's not my color," Jared said, laughing. "And I guarantee it's not Sandra's either."

He looked at Nikki.

She shrugged innocently. "I wouldn't . . ." Her voice disappeared in laughter. "I don't like reds, I like shiny. And for the record, I'd rather kiss dry lips than those."

He laughed, finally realizing he'd been so tired he hadn't read the package.

He spent the next few minutes in the

truck-stop bathroom scrubbing his mouth with soap, hiding from the burly truckers watching with curiosity. Finally he saw no more color on the paper towel and gave up. He must have sloughed off five layers of skin cells in the process. He didn't even have the courage to buy another tube on his way out.

Nikki met him at the truck with a bottle of sports drink, a greasy hamburger, and a tube of balm. "It says right on it that it's for men. Just one thing, hand over that other junk so we can get rid of it!"

"It's already gone, and I bet those fancy cosmetic companies would have charged me an arm and a leg for a lip treatment like I just gave myself." By now he could laugh, as did the others. "I don't have any skin left, but that's another issue."

"Eat up and let's get going."

"You've been practicing," he said to Nikki as they bladed under the steel-beam bridge.

She shimmied past him. "I like these wider wheels. I spent a little more time practicing while you were at work last week. Life gets pretty boring when you have one assignment and time off to get in shape for it, so I bladed every evening, too."

"Dedicated, I like that . . ." He liked a lot about Nikki, more every day. "I read your article this morning. You're doing a nice job with the story."

She shrugged. "Gary probably rewrote it. I got it to him early last night. What road are we looking for?"

He pulled the directions from his pocket. "Jerry Murphy. It turns into Overton, which is what we'll take north to Colorado Springs."

"If you'll let me go to a mall this evening to get something a little more appropriate for church services, I'll go with you tomorrow," she said, catching him off guard. "I just wouldn't be comfortable attending services like this, no matter what you say." She tugged at the T-shirt.

"Let you? I thought you didn't like shopping."

"I don't like shopping at resorts. And I *didn't* need to shop for anything that day," she explained. "Tonight, I have a mission. No pun intended."

"Fine, we'll shop if it will make you more comfortable." And if she needed to dress up in order to go to church, he'd even pay — whatever it took.

Traffic was getting lighter and the road narrower as they left the city. Jared kept the truck behind them, pulling off the highway when he felt traffic was too close to flow safely around them all.

"It's certainly cooler than it has been," Nikki commented. "I must not be working hard enough."

"Don't worry, we'll have some rolling hills in a bit, and then we'll have a nice steep climb tomorrow." Colin wasn't looking forward to the climb into Denver. "I'm not sure which would be more difficult, Monument Hill with the steep climb or Black Forest, where it's one long steady climb."

"This is much prettier, and there's a lot less traffic."

Wind gusts prevented conversation, but offered cooler, cleaner, nonpolluted breathing, which helped ward off the wheezing Colin had fought to control yesterday. Even with the balm on his lips, Colin pressed them closed for an extra safety measure from the drying wind. He spotted a wide pull-off and hurried ahead to ask Nikki if she was ready to take a water break. He tapped her on the shoulder and she turned too quickly, crumpling to the ground and rolling to a stop in the midst of a patch of thistle and scrub oak.

He scrambled down the side of road, careful to stay on his own feet. "I didn't mean to startle you."

She yanked the knee guard off, straightened her knee and flexed it again. "Ow-ee." She grimaced. "There's a sharp pain in my knee. What did you want, anyway?" She gently probed her knee, jumping when she touched the outer side.

"I was going to tell you to pull over for lunch. Sorry. Let me take a look." He rolled her pant leg above the knee and found the culprit: a thorn had wedged into her skin. He noted the scar from her surgery, which concerned him even more. What if she had twisted her knee and reinjured her leg? "You have a splinter, but your knee's already red and puffy. It can't be from this fall."

"It's been sore for a day or so. I guess it's from the last one. I must have hit it just right today."

He pressed on her knee and wiggled her ankle holding her leg in place. "Does that feel okay?"

She pulled her leg away from his embrace. "It's a little stiff and sore. It's not used to quite this much strain, but it's not injured, if that's what you're worried about. I'll be back up to speed in no time."

The sky had turned gray and rain began to fall. "Here, let's get to the trailer and I'll see if I can get that splinter out."

She took his hand and quickly steadied

herself on the skates. Colin grabbed her knee guard, hesitant to let go of her. The truck and trailer were already stopped in the pull-off ahead and Sandra was running toward them. "Is everyone okay?"

"Other than feeling like a porcupine, I'm fine. Ouch, Colin, there are more thorns in my arm."

He let go and lifted it closer, plucking the larger ones from her shirt. "You may as well just take this one off. It's going to take hours to pick them all off." He pinched her sleeve and lifted it away from her skin. "Does that help?"

She shrugged, wiggling her entire body. She tugged at her pant leg, then the waist of her shirt. "Oh, they're all over. Sandra, could you find my bag? I'm going to have to change before I can go any farther."

"Are there tweezers, alcohol and a needle in the first-aid kit? She has a splinter, too." He held her hand as they sidestepped up the slope to the highway, waiting for a line of cars to pass before they climbed to the top.

Once they were inside the pickup, the rain began in earnest, and Colin gently dug the splinter from her leg. "This is a little more closeness than I expected," Nikki said.

Sandra offered a smile of empathy. "Be glad it's him doing the surgery and not me."

"You can say that again," Jared exclaimed. "She's like a rototiller when she gets a needle in her hand."

Nikki's eyes opened wide. "You're doing just great, Colin."

He eyed her, hoping she didn't have too many more prickles to be dug out. It could get a little awkward. "I think we have all of this one. When we check into a hotel tonight, be sure to scrub it really well with soap and put some antiseptic on it." He rubbed his hand over it firmly. "Feel any of the splinter now?"

"No. It feels better. Thanks." She pulled her leg back to her side of the bench seat and handed him a sandwich. "So, are we going to finish out today on bicycle?"

"Why don't you ride in here the rest of today? I'm sure Mr. Chapman won't have any problem with it under the circumstances. In fact, I think he'd have a lot to say if I pushed you and risked injuring your knee again."

"I'm okay . . ." she started to argue, when Jared interrupted her.

"I agree with Colin, it's best to ice it now, just in case. If it's okay tomorrow you'll be that much stronger. We'll just follow Colin more slowly and let you keep your eye on him, make sure he doesn't miss a step."

"I don't think that's the real reason Grandfather wanted me with him at all times."

"Really? And what was his reason?" Jared asked, a light of humor in his eyes.

Colin tapped her leg and shook his head. "Just watch the road, Jared. Let us worry about her grandfather's motives."

When they stopped, Sandra fixed her an ice pack for her leg. "Don't let his bad attitude about money bother you, Nikki. He'll get past that soon enough."

"Time will tell."

Colin finished this leg of the relay on his own, pulling into Colorado Springs just as the rain got an icy feel to it. Nikki had used the opportunity to write her article for the next day. They stopped at the parking lot of the Citadel Mall and loaded his bicycle. He peeled the waterproof pants and rain jacket off and left them in the trailer.

"As long as we're here, why don't we run inside and get you an outfit for church. These two can find us a couple of rooms for the night and then maybe we could go out for a late supper after we've cleaned up."

Sandra smiled. "Don't worry about us, we wouldn't mind separate dinners. And I'm certain Mr. Chapman would approve as well."

* * *

"Here, let me take care of that," Colin offered when he saw Nikki pull out a credit card. After all, she would have come prepared if he'd told her ahead of time.

"You will not pay. I felt guilty enough accepting the gift card for the barbecue accident." She handed her card to the clerk. "Don't worry, I have my own account. I don't believe in carrying cash. Not when I walk back and forth from the newspaper to my car in that neighborhood."

"Why don't you park in the executive lot?" he asked when the clerk turned to talk to another customer while Nikki's card was processing.

"I park where the majority of the staff parks. I want to fit in, remember?" She signed the receipt and picked up her bag. "You don't 'fit in' by parking in the executive parking garage."

He admired her attempts to set aside the privileges of her childhood. "Do you miss the comforts you grew up with?"

She shrugged. "A few things. Like a car that I don't have to wrestle to unlock at six in the morning with panhandling drunks offering to help. I didn't expect it to be so difficult to keep my family life private in such a large city. I never thought about it meaning

I couldn't go out to dinner with Grandmother and Grandfather for fear of someone seeing us and asking questions. And I never thought about how difficult it would be to tell people after working with them for months."

"It wouldn't have been easy to go into the job as his granddaughter either." Colin took hold of her hand. "Are you happy with the relationships you have at work? Are you ready to tell them now?"

"Not really. Other than Misty, I haven't had time to get to know anyone. She has a young family, so we haven't had much in common besides trying to lose weight and work."

"Why are you trying to lose weight? You look just right," he said with a quick smile. "Unless you're still dreaming of a dancing career, and then I would really worry about you."

"I might like to teach dancing one day, but dreams of a professional career died long ago. Besides, I'm not very fond of working nights, as it turns out. It's hard to get involved with the general population." She thought a moment, then added, "Come to think of it, I just don't seem to fit in anywhere."

Colin had been through the same issues

since he'd started at the Christian radio station. "The night shift gives one a different perspective on the world. Is working at the paper even what you want to do?"

She didn't answer, just shrugged.

"There's nothing wrong with trying something outside your interests. Sometimes we even find we like it. Ten years ago I would have laughed if someone had suggested I work at a Christian radio station."

"You weren't a Christian then?"

"Yeah, I was raised in a Christian family, went to Sunday school and church every week, accepted God into my life as a young teenager. But the extent of my witness was at Vacation Bible School every summer.

"I hadn't faced many of the challenges in life that made me lean on and turn to God."

"And now you have?" Nikki asked.

"There were a lot of growing pains during my baseball career. Temptations I'd never dreamed existed when I was growing up in a conservative mountain town. I watched men slide from the top of their dreams into bankruptcy and substance abuse. I lost a close childhood friend to cancer the same summer I had my injury. And my parents almost lost their home and livelihood in the fires of 2000. And after we'd lost it once before to the economy, I just couldn't let that happen again."

"I'm sorry, Colin. I didn't mean to sound glib about it. Life is full of challenges and disappointments."

"It is if you let it be. That's when I realized how important it is to keep hold of the anchor. Playing ball didn't seem real important after seeing what others were going through."

Nikki leaned lightly into him, tilting her face toward him. "When we go to dinner tonight, there's something I want to talk to you about."

"What is it?"

"Not now," she said, looking around. "When we're alone."

Chapter Nineteen

Nikki had polished her article in record time and sent it off to Gary. He encouraged her to pick up the morning *Gazette* to find out the full scoop on the land purchase. All seemed to be going smoothly. She showered and dressed in the new slacks and sweater that she had purchased for church, then called Colin to let him know she was ready to go to dinner.

They met in the hotel lobby and walked down the block to an Italian restaurant in a light drizzle. Colin had come prepared for Sunday services and wore dress slacks and a polo shirt. She couldn't help but smile. She'd only seen him in street clothes a couple of times before. Most of the time they had both been wearing baggy athletic gear and T-shirts that quickly became drenched with perspiration.

It was much more difficult to ignore his good looks when he had just showered and smelled like the woods after a rain. "I can't believe how much colder it is than a couple of hours ago," Nikki commented, tugging her new tweed jacket closer.

"I hate to tell you this, but it's supposed to get worse before it gets better. There's snow in the forecast for tomorrow night and Monday morning. Slim chance, but a chance nonetheless."

"You're joking! It's September!"

"I'm afraid not. It's a good thing we're staying off the interstate, it's supposed to hit there midafternoon tomorrow. I'm wondering if we should try to wait it out a day or try to make it to Parker before it arrives."

"I have a few layers with me. And if we had to we could always stop by our houses on our way through Denver for more clothes. For that matter, Grandfather would understand if we needed a weather delay."

Colin opened the door to the restaurant, lightly brushing his hand on her back as she walked past him. After all they had been through, the gesture shouldn't have rattled her, but it did. Especially when his hand lingered on her waist as they approached the hostess.

"Just two, an out-of-the-way booth, if you have one," he said in that husky tone so unlike his radio voice.

The hostess seated them in a corner away from the crowd. Artificial plants and bottled vegetables lined the walls separating the tables, allowing them even more privacy. Nikki was shocked when Colin asked if he could sit next to her.

"Sure," she said as she slid over.

"I hope you don't mind. It sounded like you wanted to talk about something personal, and I hate yelling across a table. It seems like the minute you say something private, the entire room gets quiet and everyone hears what you didn't want anyone to know."

She felt the same way, but she wasn't quite expecting this reaction from him. She hoped he didn't mistake her purpose for wanting to talk to him.

Nikki looked at the menu, but her mind was stuck on Colin and what his reaction would be to her surprise. When the waitress arrived to take their order, Colin ignored the petite woman in the tight hip-huggers and even tighter T-shirt. Instead, he turned his attention totally to Nikki and what she wanted to order. His reaction was so blatant that Nikki couldn't resist teasing him when they were alone again. "What was that about?"

His guilty smile told her he wasn't used to being caught. "I must be losing my finesse. Either that or you're just more attuned to me than you're willing to admit." His eyes met hers in a loving glance. "I wanted to make it clear who I'm here with."

She laughed, and Colin seemed indignant. "I'm flattered, but I've never seen any man shy away from a cute young waitress before."

Colin leaned his elbow on the table and rested his forehead on his thumb. His cheeks rose with the width of his smile. "Then your dates were idiots not to give you their full attention. Guess that's why you're here with me tonight. I don't want to look at anyone else."

Nikki didn't know how to respond to that one. "Well, now I'm a little on the warm side." She pulled her jacket off and tucked it between her and the wall. "If you were one of my old boyfriends, I'd know you were in need of financial help after a comment like that."

"I'm not, to both of those," he said, without malice. "Okay, how much longer are you going to torment me, wondering what it is that you wanted to talk to me about?"

She wrung her hands. Colin was giving her all of his attention, and she was going to disappoint him. Should she wait?

"Well?"

Nikki leaned lightly into him and said it

before she lost her courage. "Will you help me to know God better? I want Him in my life every day."

Colin's expression brightened beyond what she could have ever imagined. "Of course I will. That's the best news I've heard all week."

"Really? I was worried you might have thought it was something about us."

"First things first, and this is far more important."

Nikki had never felt as confident about anything in her life as she did accepting Christ into her life, yet sharing that with someone new was a risk she couldn't believe she was taking. "I know this probably seems sudden," she said, "but it isn't really. I've had so much time to think while we've been on this relay. Grandmother and Grandfather have wanted me to go to church with them." Suddenly she wondered if she'd totally misunderstood Grandfather's purpose for this entire project.

Colin took hold of her hand and kissed it. She was relieved to find the attraction wasn't only in her heart. "And you couldn't, because of your secret. Your life is going to be so different when you go back to the paper. You're going to be a changed woman."

She hadn't thought about that yet, and she wasn't going to now. She had more important things to enjoy right now. "My coworker, Misty, talks about her faith, and Jared and Sandra haven't said as much as they've demonstrated through their relationship with each other. And, of course, you've made quite an impression the last few weeks. I see and feel a peace within all of you. This last month has changed my life, Colin. I want to know Him personally."

He stared at her with a look of shock, then broke out laughing. "I didn't expect it to happen so soon," he said in a husky whisper.

"As I said, you set the final example I needed. Maybe Grandfather wasn't wanting to be a matchmaker as much as to lead me to someone who could show me the joy of living for Christ."

"If I know Ellis, he's been praying for you since he found out about your mother's pregnancy. He's a good man." Colin pulled her to him and wrapped his arms around her. "Either way, I think we both came out winners."

She relished the feel of his strong and gentle embrace. She felt truly cherished, as she hadn't since she was a young child. Despite the feeling of comfort, she was worried about him and couldn't think of her own happiness. "Are you feeling okay, Colin?"

"Yeah, still a little tired, but I'll catch up on sleep tonight." He smiled, and she could see the dark circles around his eyes that she hadn't noticed before. Was it the soft lighting, or were they slightly sunken?

She stared at him and he took his arm from behind her. "Colin?" He reached for his glass of water and drained the glass. "Are you really feeling okay?"

"Can't we stop the interviewing for one night?" he said, a definite tone of annoyance in his voice.

"Is it wrong to show concern for someone I'm falling in love with? Because if it is, I guess I've been mis—"

He stopped her sentence with a kiss. Despite the gentleness of it, her emotions skidded out of control.

"Does that convince you that I'm not coming down with a cold or something? After all, I know how you feel about spreading germs. I even gargled for you."

"That was very thoughtful," Nikki said as she kissed him again.

"Selfish is more like it. I thought you were going to tell me something else tonight, and I guess when I finally heard you say it, I lost all patience. Here you just told me you're falling in love and I can't even let you finish talking."

Nikki was terribly confused. "Unless I'm interpreting that kiss wrong, I thought . . ."

"You interpret kisses, too? Sheesh, I was apologizing for not giving you warning and for not asking permission. What did you think I meant?"

She felt her face flush and her confusion deepened. "It almost sounded like you were just trying to keep me quiet. You didn't want me asking questions, and then you just kissed me." If he weren't blocking the exit, she would have run by now.

"Nikki, precious Nikki." He lifted her chin and his eyes caressed her face. His obvious admiration of her freed her to do the same. "I wanted to tell you earlier, but I wanted it to be somewhere more special than a dusty hillside or a crowded restaurant, but patience is my weakness. I've been falling in love with you since I saw barbecue sauce dripping from your beautiful chin."

Nikki felt like the prima ballerina when she was with Colin. "Oh, so that was part of your game plan all along, huh? Torment me then tell me it was all done in love?" She'd never felt so at ease and so in love.

"Yeah, smooth, don't you think?"

Nikki didn't want this evening to end. "It

was something to tell your grandchildren one day." The waitress had given up on stealing Colin's attention from Nikki, quietly serving dinner and refilling their water glasses, then moving on to flaunt her lithe body for a table of college frat boys nearby.

"So, you think there is hope of the two of us telling that story together one day?"

He stole her breath away. There were so many things he didn't know about her, and yet their feelings were laps ahead of where they should be after just a few weeks. She nodded hesitantly, not wanting to seem too eager. "I think it's a good possibility." She could easily imagine sharing her life with someone as gentle and considerate as Colin Wright. Though a husband like Colin wasn't part of her past dreams, he was now. And if it didn't work out between them, at least God had given her an example of good husband material. She would thank Him every day for giving her the courage to wait for love.

"I admit, I struggled with my feelings for you because of your money. Then there were your religious beliefs. And then I realized I'm still overly cautious of repeating previous mistakes. I'll try harder not to be so judgmental. Sometimes things don't happen in our own timing, and . . ." Colin looked down at their intertwined fingers. "This time, I was caught totally off guard. Falling in love with you was the last thing I expected."

"And when you love someone you're honest with them," she said firmly. "And I've learned my lesson."

Over dinner and then dessert, they shared a marathon of family stories and past experiences. "There's one other thing, Colin. Those flowers that were delivered that night . . ."

His body stiffened. "Whatever you say, please don't tell me they were from your boyfriend."

She pulled him closer. "A jealous ex-fiancé. I walked out on our wedding three years ago. We were barely friends, let alone in love."

"Then why were you going to marry him?"

Nikki took a deep breath to clear her memory. "I'd dropped out of dance school because of my leg, had no clue what I wanted to do, was very depressed, and Rory looked like a beacon through the fog. For a few months, I thought someone really cared about my happiness."

"And your parents were going to let you go through with it?"

"They were behind it. They thought he'd take such good care of me. He played the part quite well in front of them. He was caring and attentive when anyone else was around. Then Daddy gave him a job, just like something out of the movies. When I told my parents I couldn't go through with it, Mother was too worried about what the guests would think to care if I sold my soul . . ." Nikki struggled to finish the last sentence.

Colin squeezed her hand. "Don't stop there. What happened to make you decide it wasn't right?"

"Grandmother Chapman had a talk with me, that's what. But I was so afraid . . ." She smiled. "I didn't gather the courage to call it off until an hour before the wedding."

"Any regrets?"

She recalled Rory's hot temper and bit her lower lip. "Saying yes in the first place. He was so certain I'd come begging him to take me back."

She wasn't sure what reaction she'd expected, but she hadn't expected him to pull away now. "Colin?"

"Why is he back now?"

She shrugged. "I don't know, I haven't talked to him. Don't worry, I won't be changing my mind."

"So is he trying to get you back? Is he still mad at you and trying to get revenge, or what?" With each possibility, Colin's voice got lower. She wasn't sure if he was angry or simply worried.

Nikki stared at Colin. "I don't know, and I don't care. I have no intention of contacting him."

"You've already figured out that there are people who take advantage of the wealthy, but there are some who will do anything to avenge themselves, too." He pushed their dessert plates to the farthest corner of the table. "Did you keep the card from the flowers?"

"It wouldn't do any good, it didn't give a name."

"Then how'd you know they were from him?" His brow furrowed, and Nikki felt oddly reassured by his concern.

She had tried, unsuccessfully, to drown her fear of Rory, and it almost startled her more to have someone reinforce those feelings. She couldn't worry her grandparents about it, and none of her old friends would understand; they'd assumed all of their lives that Nikki and Rory would eventually live greedily ever after. "Because they were just like the ones from our wedding. The card said, 'Happy Anniversary.' "

"But you said you didn't get married," Colin mumbled. "I don't know, Nikki. It doesn't sound like he's just dropping by to say hello. Maybe it's time you called the police."

"No," she answered, too quickly. Colin looked as startled as she felt. Before he could question her defiance she was determined to explain. Her current acquaintances would never believe such a bizarre story from quiet, reserved Nikki Post. Would Colin?

If it changed their friendship, then God hadn't meant for this relationship to go anywhere. She might as well find out now. "He probably just wants to make me think I'm missing a storybook romance."

"With him?"

She shrugged. "He was a spoiled youngest son, and figured the two of us could just lavish each other with expensive gifts and rake in our inheritances. He is now an unemployable stockbroker. According to my father he got a bit greedy with his clients."

The smile disappeared from Colin's lips. "But it still doesn't explain why he's back. Do you think he's jealous?"

"I really just think he's run out of friends and realizes every year what he could have had." She hesitated. Maybe Colin was right, maybe she should be letting someone else know about his calls. "I'm just not sure Rory even cares about me enough to be jealous."

"Maybe he just doesn't want you to be happy."

"That's certainly a possibility." She shrugged.

Colin pulled her close, wishing they weren't sitting in a busy restaurant where anyone could overhear. "Did he hurt you?" he whispered.

"Once, but it wasn't nearly as painful physically as it was emotionally. He said he was sorry later that day, and brought me all sorts of gifts for weeks afterward, trying to convince me to keep quiet. That's when I went to talk to my parents." She spoke in a tremulous whisper, and then she stopped.

This was no place to be sharing this kind of information. He motioned for the waitress and asked for the check. "Put your coat on, Nikki, let's go back to the hotel to finish this conversation."

When they reached the hotel, though, Nikki refused to say anything more about Rory or her engagement.

"I don't want to let you go to your room like this, Nikki. Who knows how late Jared and Sandra will be, and I'm not comfortable leaving you alone. But still, it wouldn't be wise to go to your room alone right now."

She smiled for the first time in an hour. "I'll be fine. I have church to look forward to, and I hope I haven't frightened you away. I really just wanted to explain that the flowers were not a welcome gift from some other man in my life. They went directly to the trash."

"I appreciate knowing that. But I am concerned for you." He pulled her close to his side and led her down the hall to the stairs. "Have you told your grandfather that this guy has contacted you again?"

He felt her body tense in his arms. "We thought Rory was out of our lives. I'm not going to let him steal my joy, that's probably what he wants." She looked into Colin's eyes and he knew she was very much in the present again. "For the first time in a very, very long time, I feel good about myself, Colin. I have the Lord as my Savior and protector, I'm figuring out I don't have to do everything to please my family, and for now at least, I have you. Life couldn't get much better." Standing on her tiptoes, she brushed her lips against his rough chin. "Thank you for a wonderful evening, Colin," she whispered. She backed herself onto the first step, bringing them eye-to-eye. “I’m sorry I ruined it by mentioning Rory, but I wanted to be the one to tell you, so you’ll know the truth.”

Colin wanted to believe that Nikki was stronger than she had been then, and that her desire to live for the Lord was sincere.

Chapter Twenty

They were in church the next morning when Nikki received the first phone call. She quickly turned her phone off, but Colin could tell something was wrong. As soon as the service ended she wanted to leave.

"I wanted to introduce you to . . ."

Nikki looked at him with a silent plea.

"Nikki, what's wrong?" he said quietly.

"It was Rory," she whispered into his ear. "That means he had to have talked to Grandfather. My parents don't even have this number, it was assigned through the newspaper. I'm going to go to the restroom and listen to his message."

"Can't it wait a few more minutes? I want to be there."

She bolted as soon as the music stopped. By the time he made his way through the crowd and visited with his friend, Nikki was nowhere to be found. He hated to worry her grandfather, but that was the only person he could think of to call, without involving the police.

"Maybe she took a taxi back to the hotel," Sandra suggested. "You don't have to assume the worst."

He wanted to share his reasons for worrying, but didn't want to make matters worse. He called the hotel and asked if she had gone back there. They hadn't seen her, but rang her room anyway. There was no answer. Either she wasn't quite there yet, she'd deliberately wanted to be alone for some reason, or something had gone terribly wrong. "Sandra, would you check the women's restrooms again?"

She nodded. "I'll try, but I opened every door and checked every stall the first time."

"I'll check the men's restrooms, if you really think that's necessary," Jared offered.

"She wanted a quiet place to listen to her phone messages. I'll check the classrooms."

He finally found Nikki in the small chapel, sitting in the back pew. He stepped into the hallway and called Sandra to let her know before approaching Nikki. Colin walked back into the chapel and cleared his throat. Nikki didn't move. He crossed his arms over his chest and leaned against the oak pew. "I hope you have a good explanation for scaring me half to death."

She closed her eyes and shook her head. "I needed time to think — alone. He needs money. And I don't know what to do." Nikki leaned forward with her elbows on her knees and dropped her head into her hands. “I need you and Jared and Sandra to go on without me, Colin. I shouldn’t be associated with the relay right now.”

“What does Rory have to do with your involvement with the relay?” Colin rested his hand on his hip.

“I don’t want to take any chances. He is beyond angry, and when he lashes out, you never know where the pieces will land. Somehow his new employer found out he’d falsified both his diploma and his broker’s license. He thinks I told them.”

“So, because he did something illegal, he wants you to pay?” Colin couldn’t imagine anything so terrible that it could frighten her away from doing something she believed in.

“I’m sure the thought of going to the officials is frightening, Nikki, but I really think it’s time. He made that decision, you didn’t.”

“He’ll find a way out of any charges, and then he’ll be twice as angry. I just don’t want to hurt the chances of a new shelter going through. I don’t want anyone to find out. And I don’t want your reputation hurt. You have a promising career, Colin, and something like this could . . .”

Silent tears fell, and Colin slid into the

pew next to her and kissed her forehead. "I'm sure your family would understand, Nikki. Your grandparents supported you walking out on the guy, they have opened doors for you to start over here, and besides that, surely your parents realize now what Rory was doing and would never turn their backs on you."

"I'm an embarrassment to them. Rory's in Denver and wants money to get out of the country." All of Nikki's insecurities flooded out, and Colin gave up trying to reason with her and just let her vent her frustrations until the tears finally stopped. "And I don't want to risk hurting you or the shelter, Colin. I'll explain to Grandfather, but I can't let this hurt you."

"It's not going to hurt me, but it's time to call the police, before he does something dangerous."

He knew as well as the Lord was His Son that the truth didn't really matter in cases like this once the ugly allegations hit the wires. Public opinion made the ultimate judgment.

"Let's take a break today, stay here, say we're waiting for the weather to clear."

"No, you go ahead. I'm going to call my parents. Maybe their lawyer can stop Rory since we know where he is now."

"Nikki, I want you to think of something while you prepare to talk to your family. Remember that even Jesus knew scandal from the moment he was conceived of the Holy Spirit. His parents lived with the shame of her unwed motherhood, and yet Joseph and Mary put their trust in God to lead them through every day of Jesus' life. I have to believe that they never shirked the honor He bestowed on them. If they can handle it, we can. After all, He even tells us that of those who have been given many blessings, much more will be expected. The life of a Christian isn't easy, but His grace promises everlasting rewards."

"Couldn't God have given me a few days to prepare for the big leagues?" She offered a weak smile.

"We're a team, Nikki. God had that planned long before we did, too. His foresight is pretty awesome. Let's take a minute to pray, shall we?"

Nikki held Colin tight while he prayed for strength and protection from the enemy as they prepared for the battle. While they drove back to the hotel, he filled Jared and Sandra in.

"Would all of you stay with me when I call my family?" Nikki asked, surprising Colin.

They moved to a hotel with tighter security and larger accommodations so they could avoid any further intrusion to their privacy. The two-bedroom suite also offered the comforts of a sofa and easy chairs for the long day ahead.

Nikki remained strong while she made the conference call to her parents and grandparents, then, when the call was over, she collapsed next to Colin on the sofa.

"Grandfather is going to put a short article about the delay in the newspaper, blaming the weather. Now I hope it snows a foot to support the story. You journalists think alike, I guess."

Colin smiled, then kissed her forehead. "Why don't you watch the snow, maybe it will put you to sleep."

Nikki moved to the girls' room and covered up with the down comforter while Colin called her grandfather from the living room. When he returned, she was sound asleep. He and Sandra and Jared flipped back and forth through all of the local stations for any hint of Rory's capture or his breaking his promise to give them a day to pay him off.

When the phone chirped, Colin snatched it up so quickly it didn't make it through the first ring. "Hello."

"Is this Colin?" After Colin confirmed his

identity, Nikki's father introduced himself and filled him in on the difficulty they'd had reaching their lawyer. "I just want to thank you for insisting Nikki call us. The FBI has been investigating Rory clandestinely for years, and he also accused me of turning him in."

Colin's heart raced as he considered admitting to her father that he had contacted his own private investigator to start researching Rory the night before. "I didn't know the full extent of the problem last night when Nikki told me about his contact with her. You can contact my investigator if you'd like to. He has gathered some information about his location. Other than that, there isn't much he can do."

"You didn't trust Nicole?"

"No, sir, I didn't trust Rory. I had no idea why he was contacting her, but it didn't sound like a good situation. I love your daughter, and I'm doing everything within my power to take care of her."

"I appreciate that, Colin. Ellis says he couldn't have picked a finer man to go through this with her."

Colin laughed at the irony of the situation. "He and I are going to have a nice visit when this is over. I'll call the investigator and ask him to fax you copies of everything he has so far. What's the number to your fax, and where can he reach you?" Colin wrote down her father's information, noting that he would have to keep this for future reference. He'd need to be scheduling a visit with him in the near future, as well.

The evening progressed without any excitement, and Nikki slept through every phone call. Finally at midnight, everyone turned in and prepared for the next day.

By late afternoon the Feds had tracked Rory down and made the arrest.

Colin watched the clouds move to the east and blue sky appear. He'd hardly slept at all last night. "There's no sense in us waiting here on pins and needles. Why don't we get going and burn off some of this tension?"

Jared looked at Nikki. "The roads look like they're drying out. You should have no trouble on the highway. That's the nice part about early storms like this." Jared rambled on as if this were any normal day.

She looked nervously at Colin. "I guess we have to get as far as Denver, anyway. We may as well get started." The closeness they had shared during the emotional crisis had faded once she found out Colin had called her parents. Nikki kept a cool distance between them. While her adrenaline level appeared to have taken a dive, his couldn't have been higher.

Twenty miles into the trek the clear sky disappeared and Colin began to feel the effects of too many sleepless nights. With the cool weather, he should be making better time than when it was hot, but each mile seemed to get more difficult. "Let's take a break," he yelled. Nikki was only a few yards ahead of him, but didn't seem to hear. The few yards seemed more like miles when he tried to catch up and ride beside her.

Drifts spilled through the snow fences protecting the livestock in the pasture across the highway from the brunt of Colorado's winters. It served as a reminder that no matter how man tried to maintain control, God still had the final say. *"Lord, you are so alive and with me today."* Colin took several deep breaths, unable to stop the coughs. Nikki turned immediately.

When he finally caught up to Nikki, they were looking ahead to a steep climb and he knew it was useless to stop now. He unzipped his waist pack and pulled out his inhaler. *"You, Lord, have more power than this little canister. If it be your plan, heal my lungs and let me finish this race."* He coughed again, and thought of the parable of the mustard seed. How many foolish men had arrived at the pearly gates of heaven and received a reminder from God that even medicine was His creation. He administered another dose and breathed the medicine deep into his lungs.

When they reached the crest of the high plains they could see the dark clouds encroaching on the city. Nikki pulled off into a school parking lot and waited. "Are you okay?"

Colin nodded. "Looks like the tail of this storm is whipping back around."

"Why don't we rest here tonight?"

Colin shook his head. "I'm going to keep going. We only have four more days to finish."

Jared pulled to a stop beside them. "Why don't you take a break?"

Nikki stared at him with a frown creasing her beautiful face. "I'm fine," Colin said. "Let's take the blades through Parker and stop for a hot meal there."

"No," she said. "Why don't we just stop, Colin? Grandfather will give you the money anyway, you know that. And if he doesn't, I will."

"And give up in the middle? Take the easy way out? Not a chance. I like to win fair and square."

Jared had shifted to Park and was putting

the bicycles into the trailer while Nikki and Colin sat on the tailgate changing into the Rollerblades. "I want to know what's wrong with you, Colin."

Her anger caught him off guard. "You have some right to lecture me on watching out for yourself. I said I'm fine."

"You've been coughing and breathing funny. What is it?"

"I have allergies. They are acting up, but I'm taking my medicine."

"Allergies? You were coughing, not sneezing. And besides that, we're in the middle of a snowstorm, what's left in the air that can be causing problems today?"

He looked at her strangely; she was beginning to think the problem must be with her. "What are you allergic to?"

"The dust and pollen we had in Pueblo must have triggered this cough, and it's why I'm taking my medicine. It's under control. And it has nothing to do with why I'm doing this marathon. Really. I'm preasthmatic, but I've never even had an asthma attack. You can ask my parents. Once we get away from this smog, it will probably improve."

She stared at him in disbelief. "Should you even be doing this?"

Colin nodded. "We're over halfway through and I only have minor symptoms.

It's just a cough. When I use the inhaler it clears right up." He took a deep breath and prayed he wouldn't cough. "See, it's working fine."

"I don't want anything to happen to you."

"Neither do I." He took her hand in his. "Neither do I."

Chapter Twenty-One

Colin stopped at his place overnight, staying barely long enough to shower, sleep and get dry clothes. Even though they had gotten away from the heavy pollution in Denver, his cough was more persistent than ever. Nikki wanted to scream. Finally they made it to Brighton, cold and soaked to the skin, despite the rain gear, and Nikki resorted to the only thing left — prayer. *"Lord, I pray you to knock some sense into this man who is too stubborn for his own good,"* she yelled.

Colin clapped for her "performance," quickly putting his hands back on the handlebars as the bike wobbled.

"You can't even drive straight." A gust of wind forced the words back into her mouth.

"Backseat drivers . . ." he mumbled.

"I heard that." She laughed in spite of the frustration. At least he still had his sense of humor. "What was that verse you preached to me about the eagle resting? You need to get some sleep so you can finish this tomorrow, Colin." Nikki rode alongside him since the traffic had all but disappeared.

"Even the drivers have sense to get off these icy roads."

Temperatures were dropping and the mist was freezing on the highway. "We're almost there."

"Where? We're at least forty miles from the next large town. There's a motel sign. Let's each get a room and finish it off tomorrow."

Colin's cough had stopped and in its place was a painful and frightening-sounding wheeze. Still he pushed on through the freezing rain.

"Please, Colin. I love you. I don't want to see you hurting like this. What are you trying to prove, that you're a martyr? God gave you more sense than to abuse your body like this."

"I need to beat this storm."

"It's dark and cold and wet. Let's stay here tonight and get an early start in the morning." She stared at him as she said this, aware that it wasn't the gentle man she loved speaking. He wasn't even angry with her. In her heart she knew that. His body had switched from flight mode to fight. And he was fighting not only with his heart, but also his soul.

Finally he agreed, collapsing in the hotel as soon as his head hit the pillow. Though they had all agreed to let him sleep as long as possible, Colin was awake and ready to leave before noon. The roads were wet and slushy from the freezing rain and salted streets. Everything for the last three hours had been as miserable and challenging as anything she'd experienced. Her father and grandfather insisted she continue with the relay and stay with Colin while they dealt with Rory. She struggled with leaving her problem to anyone else, but knew that they could deal with the legal aspects of the issue far better than she ever could.

Every hour Colin paused for a drink of hot tea and a bite to eat, then topped it off with a whiff of his inhaler. They tied a scarf around his nose and mouth to prevent him from breathing the icy-cold air. He quit conversing as they rode through Greeley late the next day when the stench of the feedlots and sugar-beet factory forced him to fight for every breath.

"Colin, there are no other places to stop after Greeley. Come on, you can't keep going."

He pushed her hand aside and shook his head in silence. Nikki's body ached. She could only imagine how badly Colin's hurt. He'd not slept half as much as she had in the previous week. And with his illness, what little he had slept hadn't done much good.

Her intermittent prayers became one long conversation with God as she struggled to understand why Colin wouldn't take a break. *Make him stop, Lord. Please . . .*

Temperatures felt as though they had dropped even more as they inched toward the final stretch. Rain turned to snow and Colin's breathing sounded like Old Man Winter's.

"I hate you for doing this, Colin Wright. I hate you!" she cried finally. "If you loved me and the God that you serve, you'd humble yourself enough to stop before you kill yourself."

He didn't even acknowledge that he'd heard her. He pushed the pedals of the bicycle harder, weaving back and forth across the lanes of the barren highway. The darkness engulfed them, brightened only by the occasional hint of a mercury light from a farmhouse. Icy snowflakes felt as if they were piercing her skin.

She watched in disbelief as Colin crawled under the gate blocking the highway and dragged his cycle underneath.

"Colin, don't be an idiot," Jared moaned as he jumped out of the truck and followed him through the barrier on foot. "It's against the law to ignore a closed highway."

He turned to the women and shrugged. They couldn't help but smile. Even Colin's best friend was grasping at straws.

Colin struggled to find his footing and get back on the bike. Finally a few feet down the road he simply collapsed and the three of them fell to his side.

"Colin!" Sandra shook him and his eyes opened. "Call an ambulance, Jared. He's too weak to fight us any more. Maybe they can send a helicopter."

"Nikki, get his inhaler," she said as she loosened the scarf from his icy face. Nikki saw that the fabric was frozen around his mouth from the moisture of his breathing. She leaned over him, exhaling to warm it enough to take it off. Every other breath she uttered words of encouragement and fear. "Don't you dare leave me without fulfilling our dreams, Colin. You promised me grandchildren, and I mean to collect."

Jared laughed. "Now that ought to scare him back to life," he joked as he returned from the truck. "The dispatcher is calling the local police officer. He'll meet us at that diner a few miles back." Jared raised Colin's shoulders, wrapped his arms under Colin's armpits, unable to lock his hands over Colin's chest because of the bulky coat. He heaved his friend's listless body off the ground and dragged him to the truck. He put Colin in the front seat, and Nikki and Sandra squeezed into the jump seat in back. "The owner will let us stay there until the ambulance arrives. In the meantime, a nurse is going to see if she can get to the diner with a nebulizer."

Nikki reclined Colin's seat and buckled him in. Tears streamed down her face and she nuzzled her face to his over the back of the seat. "I didn't mean what I said back there, Colin," she whispered. "I don't hate you. I was just so upset and desperate." He opened his eyes with a panicked look when the warm air hit his face. He started breathing faster and then the cough began again. "We have to do something for him!" Jared spun the vehicle in a U-turn in the middle of the highway and took off in a hurry, spinning the tires. Nikki held Colin's hand and squeezed tight. "I'm here, Colin. I'm not going to let anything happen to you."

Colin woke hours later in a dimly lit room with a tent over his bed, a mask over his nose with tubes and hoses trailing to IV towers next to the bed. "Well, I've done it up good this time," he mumbled. He hadn't died and gone to heaven, of that he was sure. His body would be healed if he'd made it that far. Nope, apparently God wasn't through with him yet. He was only in the hospital.

He turned, looking for Nikki. The last thing he remembered was her claiming to hate him. He knew better than to believe that, but he'd found out how much it took to make her angry. She'd be back.

Of course, Rory had thought that same thing, and she'd been strong enough to run. He hoped she wasn't that mad this time.

She'd probably just gone to get a bite to eat. She'd be back and then they'd finish the race. His eyes drifted closed again, and he felt a soft warmth just thinking of her by his side. A cool mist reminded him of how sick he really was. Though his chest was still tight, it was easier to inhale. He closed his eyes to have a visit with God and drifted into a peaceful slumber.

When he woke again the sun shone through the tightly closed shades and he was freezing cold with what felt like a hundred pounds of blankets over him. If he could see outside, there would probably be a rainbow, but Nikki still wasn't here. Neither were Jared or Sandra. Had something happened to them?

Colin started pressing buttons on the

bed's rail. The bed went up. The bed went down. The television came on, and the bell dinged. Finally, the one he wanted.

A young nurse in brightly patterned scrubs walked through the door. "Hi, Mr. Wright. It's good to see you awake."

"What?" he tried to ask. "What's this cold draft?"

She leaned closer and smiled. "You're getting another treatment of medicine. It's almost done."

From inside the tent her voice was muffled, but he did understand enough to know he'd have to wait a few more minutes to talk to her.

She reached under the tent and hooked a clamp to his finger, then wrapped the blood pressure cuff around his bicep. "The doctor will be here in a few minutes."

"What about my friends? Do you know where they are?"

"I think they went home to get some sleep. Has anyone ever told you that you should have your head examined? What did you think you were doing, taking a chance with asthma?"

The doctor stepped through the door and scowled at the nurse. "I'll take over, Miss Jones."

She looked at the doctor and left without

a word. He introduced himself as Dr. Davis and lifted one side of the tent. "She *is* right, even though her approach needs some work."

"I needed to get to the Wyoming border. I'm . . ."

"I know who you are and all about the stunt." He wrote on Colin's charts in silence, checking the monitors occasionally.

He couldn't believe Nikki would have just left him here. Sure she was angry, but . . . Then he remembered Rory. Maybe something had gone wrong there. He tried to figure out how to change the channels on the television.

"Mr. Wright, how do you feel?"

"Much better," he said, forgoing the humorous answer that had initially come to mind. "My chest isn't tight, and the cough appears to be gone."

"That's what they all say," the doctor said as he held up a contraption and unhooked a tube from the cylinder. He explained how to use it and asked Colin to take a deep breath, then exhale as much as he could into the tube. "If you can get this arrow to the top, I'll let you go. Deal?"

Colin had his doubts. He felt good, but these little tests were always harder than they looked. "Do I get a handicap?"

"That's why you're here," he said with a smile. "I'm a sporting man, Mr. Wright. Used to compete in body-building. So I admire your dedication to your marathon, even though you were pretty close to striking out altogether. I'll play your game. Best out of three."

Colin wasn't quite sure how to take the man. "Do you know how I can get hold of Nikki, the woman I was with?" Colin asked with a sense of trepidation.

"She's on her way. You seem to be a very lucky man. I don't know a woman alive who'd have stuck with you through that."

He looked around. "She's not here yet. Maybe I'm not as lucky as you think."

The doctor smiled. "Quit stalling, and step up to the plate."

Colin took a deep breath and exhaled. The arrow only hit halfway.

"Strike one," the doctor said.

"You're not seriously going to keep me in here because of this gizmo, are you?"

"Breathe in through your nose and out your mouth. Batter up."

Colin took two deep breaths and let them out, then on the third, exhaled into the tube. He started coughing, but gritted his teeth, not about to give up until the bitter end.

"Close."

The third try he hit a home run and the doctor smiled. "Good work." He reached into the pocket of his white lab coat and pulled out a piece of paper. "I'm on the board of our local shelter. Add this to your donations." He scribbled his signature on the clipboard. "No physical exertion until you have clearance from your doctor. I want you to see this specialist at the Asthma Center in Denver. They need to set you up on a long-term treatment plan. If you're careful about it, you shouldn't have any limitations. I do think, however, that it's time to let the younger generation go for these absurd challenges."

Nikki walked through the door, Sandra and Jared behind her. "Aren't you dressed yet? We don't have much time."

"For what?" he said, motioning for her to come closer.

"We have a relay to finish."

He felt his hopes sink. "I can't. I'm not going to put us through that again. I'm sorry for the scare."

Nikki pressed her lips to his and ran her hand along his scruffy face. "Let me take care of the details this time. Okay? When I come back I want you dressed in these clothes and ready to go. No questions asked, just trust me." She handed him a huge plastic bag.

He looked at the smile on Jared's face and knew something was up. He opened the bag and found warm polar-fleece–lined sweats, a heavy wind-resistant coat, and new tennis shoes. The two women walked out of the room and Jared handed him another bag.

"I took care of the essentials, as usual. Have we got a surprise for you." With that, he too left. Colin opened the bag and laughed when he saw a bright red pair of long johns.

Ten minutes later they were headed north on Highway 85 to the Wyoming border. "So what's the big surprise?"

"You're going to have to be patient."

Silence enveloped the cab. Finally, Jared reached for the dash and turned on WWJD. The news announcer reported a change in the fight for the shelter.

"What's up?"

They pulled to a stop in Nunn. "You wait here," Nikki said with a smile. "I'll be right back."

Ahead, Colin noticed a news van parked at the café, and he knew this was going to be a day he'd never forget.

"Here you go." Colin turned and saw his final mode of transportation — a wheelchair, complete with footrests, a blanket and an oxygen tank. "We're a team, all the way," Nikki laughed.

"I think I'm going to have to marry this woman," Colin said with a smile. "Because this is a story to tell our grandchildren."

Tears welled in Nikki's eyes. "Let's start with our own kids first."

"How about your godson or goddaughter?" Jared interrupted, with his arms in the air as if he'd scored a touchdown. "We're going to beat you to parenthood."

Colin gave his friend a high five and Sandra a hug. "You just give us a chance, we'll have a hockey team in no time."

Sandra and Nikki looked at one another. "Don't get too carried away, guys. There's one detail we have yet to settle."

"What's that?"

"Someone's got to get over the threshold first. Get in," Sandra said with a chuckle.

Colin sat in the seat, realizing how close he had come to losing all of this — his life, his love and a happiness he couldn't even imagine yet — a family.

The air was cool and moist, even though the sun was turning the snow to mush on the asphalt. He hated to see Nikki working so hard to push him. He reached for the wheels and started turning.

"Oh, no, you don't." She stopped immediately. "The doctor only agreed to let us do this if you didn't move a muscle. The ambulance back there probably has a straitjacket we can use if we have to."

Nikki took short breaks, allowing Jared to spell her for a mile or so at a time. He felt so guilty, wrapped in down blankets and long underwear. He had a mask on to keep the cold air from irritating his lungs. He could hear the truck stop and Nikki return to swap places with Jared.

"Nikki," he said, his voice muffled. "I'm so sorry I've done this to you. Honestly . . ." Colin pulled the mask away from his mouth while he finished the sentence. "I've never had an asthma attack. I thought I could manage it with the inhaler."

She pressed the mask over his mouth again and pushed his hand under the blanket. "God was listening to our prayers."

"I'm almost afraid to ask what those were?"

"You should be. There were three of us, you know, so God really listened. We asked him to knock you out before you killed yourself. You were inches from home base." He could hear the emotion in her voice.

He tried to turn to look at her, but it sent the wheelchair off course when his weight shifted the balance. "Are you crying?" he asked.

There was a long silence as she pushed him around a drift blown back over after the plows had gone through this morning.

"You're right I am. You made me so mad."

"Angry. I made you angry."

"Whatever. Enough of the journalism lessons. You scared me to death, Colin."

He rode in silence for several miles, regretting that his carelessness had caused such trouble. They passed the Clown's Den in Rockport and he could see the bright colors of the people little more than a mile away at the finish line. She sniffed as they came to a long, steep hill, the final stretch to the Wyoming border. As she pushed closer, the crowd looked far too large to be only members of the press. "So, I hope this is the whole big surprise, the wheelchair ride . . ."

"Not quite."

"Have I mentioned that I don't like surprises?"

Nikki laughed. "Too late. I think you'll like this one."

Since the road was officially still closed, two of the greeters stretched a red ribbon across the highway. Colin had the pleasure of taking it with him across the state line. Nikki put on the brakes and Colin removed the mask and climbed out to a crowd of friends and co-workers from the newspaper and the radio.

Ellis Chapman sauntered over to them and the cameramen stood waiting. "Colin Wright, we're honored to have you here with us today, for more than the customary reasons." Everyone laughed. "Few people have gone to the lengths that you have to raise money for charities in the state of Colorado. It's my pleasure to present the Good Samaritan Shelters of Colorado a bond for seven hundred thousand dollars to be used to build a new shelter for needy families in the Denver area." Pictures snapped and Colin looked around, seeing people he'd never seen before. "I'm not sure if anyone has ever totaled your individual earnings and pledges for charities, Colin, but it's a world record. I want to thank the press for coming today, and since there is still a bite to this wind, we're going to get Colin and my granddaughter Nicole Post into the warmth and back to civilization."

It didn't take long for the crowds to disperse and for family to gather round Colin and Nikki. Sandra and Jared led the caravan south, while Nikki led Colin to the couple near the luxury stretch SUV. "Dad, Mom, this is Colin Wright."

"Nice to meet you in person, Colin."

He smiled. "This is the surprise, isn't it?"

Nikki glowed. "Bringing all of the family together for this became pretty important today." His parents stepped forward to give him a hug, and then Colin pulled Nikki into his arms and held her close, tears threatening to embarrass him more than the chance he'd already taken with their lives. He turned them both toward her parents. "You have the most wonderful daughter, and I'm sure that this is about the worst timing in the history of romance to ask permission to marry her, but it seems to be my day for blessings."

"We'll stand behind Nicole's decision."

Nikki leaned into him and lifted her gaze to Colin's eyes. "God blessed me the day you walked into your grandfather's office and plopped blindly into my lap, Nikki."

"Colin . . ." she said between gritted teeth. "You didn't have to mention that . . ."

Grandfather's laugh echoed across the valley.

"So I guess you don't want me to mention me dumping the plate of barbecued ribs on you, either?"

She blushed. "Not that it matters now."

He kissed her cold nose. "Now for one on myself. A few days ago, Nikki refused to let me borrow her lip balm, so I had to go and buy my own, which I did under the influence of no sleep and total exhaustion."

Tears rolled down Nikki's cheeks.

"If looking at me with bright red lips didn't frighten you away, Nikki, God has to have stripped me of my pride and wrapped you up and given you to me as a wedding gift. Will you marry me?"

"Of course I will. The last eight days and three hundred some miles have totally changed my life, thanks to you, Colin. You stopped my heart from that first humiliating moment I laid my eyes on you. If we can make it through this together, I can't wait to see what ups and downs the journey to forever will bring us through."

Dear Reader,

I am always impressed when I see Americans who volunteer their precious time to help others. Most of us serve in a way that is relatively familiar to us. Yet every now and then, God calls us to step out of our comfort zones, to "stretch our boundaries" and in return, He will richly bless us.

I often need to remind myself that God expects no more of us than He did His own Son, to reach out to others and utilize the gifts He has given us. It was extremely fun to write about Nikki and Colin, a couple who accept God's challenge to do something for others in need and find His many blessings along the way. I hope that you will enjoy their journey into their future and look forward to God's calling in your own life.

If you would like to find out more about my journey, log on to my Web site at www.carolsteward.com or contact me at P.O. Box 200286, Evans, CO 80620.

Many blessings,

Carol Steward

About the Author

CAROL STEWARD wrote daily to a pen pal for ten years, yet writing as a career didn't occur to her for another two decades. "My first key chain said, 'Bloom where you're planted.' I've tried to follow that advice ever since."

Carol, her husband and their three children have planted their roots in Greeley. Together, their family enjoys sports, camping and discovering Colorado's beauty. Carol has operated her own cake-decorating business and spent fifteen years providing full-time child care to more than one hundred children before moving on the other end of the education field. She is now an admissions adviser at a state university.

As always, Carol loves to hear from her readers. You can contact her at P.O. Box 200269, Evans, CO 80620. She would also love for you to visit her Web page at www.carolsteward.com.

The employees of Thorndike Press hope you have enjoyed this Large Print book. All our Thorndike and Wheeler Large Print titles are designed for easy reading, and all our books are made to last. Other Thorndike Press Large Print books are available at your library, through selected bookstores, or directly from us.

For information about titles, please call:

(800) 223-1244

or visit our Web site at:

www.thomson.com/thorndike
www.thomson.com/wheeler

To share your comments, please write:

Publisher
Thorndike Press
295 Kennedy Memorial Drive
Waterville, ME 04901